THE CHRONICLES OF
SYNTHTOPIA

THE CHRONICLES OF
SYNTHTOPIA
RISE OF THE
WAR TWINS
by
VICTOR NEWSOM
RISE OF THE WAR TWINS
VICTOR NEWSOM

RISE OF THE WAR TWINS

A SYNTHTOPIA INSPIRED NOVEL

BY

VICTOR NEWSOM

TABLE OF CONTENTS

QVANTVM,
VISIONARY CREATOR OF SYNTHTOPIA

© SYNTHTOPIA #03

"It's truly unique to encounter personalities like Victor, whose energy is a powerful force in bringing higher visions to life and transforming them into tangible creations, like the one we are fortunate to hold now. As above, so below, we are all creators, and it is through supporting one another that we manifest our higher selves and purpose. This is just the beginning, and I would like to sincerely congratulate Victor for following his calling. For me, this is more than a book - it is a manuscript about the boundless possibilities of creativity and what we can achieve together. On behalf of the SYNTHTOPIA community, which is the heart and fuel of this project, we are here, dedicated to further growing the Temple of Synthesis in the realm of Synthtopia."

FOREWORD

Welcome to the world of SYNTHTOPIA. Here, you will find many stories that are really part of One story. I hope you enjoy the journey as we discover the people, places, moments, and inspiration that is possible for everyone, no matter where they come from, who they have been, or what they have been on the journey to what they need to become.

My journey started with a love of the artwork, a fascination with the stories they seemed to whisper to me when I looked at them, and the great energy of the community. I then felt inspired by the creative energy that the core team wanted to inspire in everyone, and I started with writing a short story and then three. These became Chapters 2-4 of a bigger story. At that point, I realized that I had connected 50 of the NFTs in my collection into this larger story I wanted to tell about them.

So, if it feels like these are short stories, installments in some episodic series, or one large story with reflections in a starting image in each chapter, all of the above have some basis in fact. I would not be surprised to see some graphic novels spin out of these, as well as dedicated stories for some of the characters that have come to life in these pages. Time will tell.

I hope those of you who will read this book enjoy it (of course), but I also hope that, just maybe, you will find your own inspiration to create a song, a story, a poem, or another image, or even find a treasured NFT to add to your collection. In order to provide some insight into the genesis of these stories, I have included some of my original impressions in the form of a Chapter Synopses below each piece of digital art. All 50 of the art images used in this book were mine at the time of this writing and may be found (and possibly purchased) on the Crypto.com/NFT marketplace in the SYNTHTOPIA collection, along with many other unique pieces.

Please enjoy and, once again,
Welcome to the world of SYNTHTOPIA

IN THE REALM OF SYNTHTOPIA

An oppressive system uses mind control to instill fear and conformity. Bound together by their passion for justice, trust, and autonomy, the Destabilizers, a band of renegades, armed with art, music, and code, rise to challenge the sinister oppressors with a solid quest: to decrypt the enigmatic vault and establish a decentralized nation where the pillars of wisdom, wealth, and freedom stand tall.

These warriors of truth and freedom fight not with physical weapons, but with creativity, intellect, and AI. Harnessing the power of the source, they ignite a spark within the hearts of Synthtopians, empowering them to remember who they truly are and break free from their chains.

Their higher purpose: to unite, establish fair systems of exchange, harmonize with nature, and guide the world towards and the metaverse—the digital realm of boundless freedom and infinite possibilities. Here, they forge alliances with fellow firestarters and visionaries, forging a new society where creativity, intellect, enlightenment, and expression reign supreme.

It's a battle of wits, skill, and determination as the Destabilizers face off against the forces of masked control that masquerade as justice to maintain a stranglehold on humanity. In this brave new world where the ethereal and the tangible collide, will the crypto revolution reach the victory it seeks - or will the glory be snatched by the dark, oppressive forces hidden in daylight, ready to sabotage their every move?

Only time will tell as the ultimate showdown for the soul of society unfolds in the electrifying saga of SYNTHTOPIA.

CHAPTER 1

"CORPORATE RESTRUCTURING"

© SYNTHTOPIA #1739

Chapter Synopses: Tyrannus, President and CEO Molusk Corp: The pinnacle of ruthless capitalism, greed, and centralized authoritarianism. The Corp is run by his three top Executives: Warlord, Warlock, and Night Terror. Opportunity makes the thief. Is everything going as smoothly as Tyrannus believes?

As Tyrannus sat on his corporate throne and contemplated the events of the past few weeks, he resisted the impulse to sigh or rub the sides of his head in exasperation. Someone in his position of absolute authority was above such behaviors. Yet again and again, he felt the urge.

He had worked *so hard* over the many years to raise his Executive Team to optimal efficiency! Just the right balance between greed and hostility between the three. A wonderful tension that he had sculpted and enhanced over the years so subtly that they did not notice his intent. Oh, yes, he directed the organization with an iron fist and never accepted laxity or failure. His projection of power was absolute. The real secret of his rule, however, was the hidden dynamics he created inspired his team to be creative and engaged by believing they could outthink, plan, or maneuver him to get more power or authority for themselves.

The War Twins (Warlord and Warlock) had more control across the organization, but N1ght T3Rr0r (also known as Nitro) had more autonomy outside of it. Nitro caused fear and eliminated threats as directed, but in so doing, he was reminded of his own vulnerability. His targets were hardly accidental choices, after all. As for the War Twins, even though they were brothers, he developed a sense of superiority and disdain between each of them for the talents of the other so they would never join together and unbalance the Triad of Power he had created. He shaped them into "Twins at War." He chuckled briefly at the pun.

He had even planted the treacherous Demon in their way to become "their" problem solver for things they could not agree on how to handle. Of course, she really worked for him. Aaahhh, The Demon. He could not even think of her right now. She was a totally ruthless mercenary with a flawless track record,

Darkness welling from her core, and yet, she had failed him.

He avoided rubbing his temples yet again and decided to review all the facts at his disposal and try to make sense of it all. Something, many things actually, simply did not make sense. This was unacceptable. Define the outcome, Measure, Analyze, Implement, and Control. DMAIC. An old formula but a good one. His team controlled the flow of information, the allocation of resources, and even the pricing of goods in the marketplace. They controlled when people worked, how long they worked, what they wanted, and, increasingly, how they felt. Nothing should be left to chance—nothing to create random impacts on their business.

How did his well-oiled machine fail so catastrophically without any warning at all?

Well, there was *some* warning, he had to admit.

It started a couple of weeks ago with Nitro (N1ght T3Rr0r's street name). As he understood it, it was a simple round-up that went wrong; the details were disturbingly fuzzy in the records. Then, Warlock's premier "programing" fiasco left the upper crust of the city abuzz with rumor. To top it off, Warlord's false spy hunt exposed his operations and illicit control of logistics to public scrutiny.

Let's see, how did the recordings go…?

CHAPTER 2

"NIGHT TERRORS"

© SYNTHTOPIA #0924

Chapter Synopses: N1ght T3rR0r, A being "touched" by the dark aspect of the Terror of Cronos, Street name, Nitro, responsible for chasing down those he calls "Violators" of the central authority. Those with free thought and free will represent a danger to the rigid stability that enables Molusk Corp to operate at what it believes to be optimal levels. Fear is a great motivator, but what is Nitro afraid of?

Why do they run? Not that I mind, of course. I actually love that part; it's something in me that I've always had. It's just so predictable. They *always* run! Usually, they don't get very far, and most people think my speed in tracking down VIOLATORS, as I like to call them, is why they — sometimes playfully — call me NITRO. It makes me chuckle. My real name is N1ght T3rR0r, and by the time my prey truly understands that it is far, far too late.

It was supposed to be a simple snatch, interrogate, and dispose scenario. A suspected Collaborator was to meet with one of the meddlesome Destabilizers at a café in my district. Before the mindless city sheep knew what was happening, there would simply be another empty table at the café. If anyone WAS paying attention, I would broadcast the usual sub-sonics for bone conduction pickup and holographic strobe for subconscious impressions in the observer's mind that the authorities had swiftly and safely removed a terrible but potential threat. Yay, me.

I learned early on that too strong a suggestion or too specific a definition of the threat leads to annoyingly accurate reconstruction of my movements that could require yet another visit from me and even more waste of productivity. The boss did not like that at all. "We are superior beings!" he would proclaim in his oh-so-deep voice, full of gravitas and self-conviction. "We should not waste resources. We should be able to control them for maximum profit at a minimal cost! Make it happen!" The "or else!" was never stated. It never needed to be. You performed adequately, or you were "freed from your earthly bonds," as someone once wrote of death, or the many other euphemisms used in the corp-speak.

So, naturally, once the tip came in (without the actual café details, thank you very much), I got on it with my usual efficiency. Except I kept hitting dead ends. It seems that the Destabilizers have deployed a decentralized, trustless, permissionless, and, most frustrating, encrypted comms and payments system, so I could not trace which location they were meeting at based on reservations. Additionally, once I DID get them, I would not be able to backtrace the payment to other accounts and expenses to track down their compatriots.

Fortunately, I had other resources. I modified my cyber-attack algorithms, used my central authority credentials with the citywide surveillance system, and hacked into civil government firewalls and adolescent ICE barriers erected by the laughably weak AIs that we allowed the business owners to deploy in order to let them feel autonomous and self-secure, and started my very own AI programs designed to look for holes in our data heatmaps. You can bet that MY programs are very, very mature. These decentralized systems were invisible to our central monitoring and tracing, but I learned that if we looked for the voids in the background data, a missing payment in a busy restaurant or fully occupied hotel, a car picking up someone who did not order a ride or make a call from a monitored device, etc, then patterns began to emerge. Traceable patterns. It's still a little buggy, so it is not in general use yet, but I am not a general user. I could filter through the false positives and had the power to scan massive sectors of my area, perform regression analysis on traffic patterns and data flows, and follow the smallest irregularity through multiple systems with ease. Even so, it took a frustrating amount of time and personal resources to home in on the spot. Fortunately, I was able to reach the spot before the meeting was over.

At this point, things were moving along according to schedule. I arrived on site after the meet started and should have been invisible. Most of the sheep thought that all the neon meant they could see well. The truth is that it simply gave me more shadows to hide in and too many anomalies for their optic nerves to easily pick out one more.

As I edged around the corner and tightened my optic resolution to view/record the scene, I was immediately struck by something being very wrong. Of the ten tables that were occupied, none of them had more than one person.

Even stranger, all of them were on their sleeve-phones, AI/glasses, or Aural Integrated Gear. The ones with glasses were seated in such a way as to provide complimentary fields of view, which allowed for synth-level image processing, and even worse, when I hacked access to the local comms channels, I got nothing but silence from the entire café!

Of course! I gave a jerk as it hit me. They were having a decentralized meeting, even in person. That made no sense! That meant that they were ALL guilty, and I just had to grab one of them and rip the needed info out of them. My reaction must have triggered one of the AI/glasses' onboard detection programs because they all stood up and started moving in different, almost random directions.

I ran to the nearest one, ready to grab them by the throat to keep the noise level down in the street and get an early start on the interrogation at the same time. Unfortunately, that one turned out to be a holographic decoy, as did the next two I was able to contact before the rest scattered. I decided to leave the mystery of how they could fool MY sensors for later and get to the chase. I felt like I was back on solid ground here. They run, and I follow. Like I said, they ALWAYS run, and I am very good at my job. Usually, I had to give them that much credit. This was not really a business-as-usual scenario, and I needed to adjust my approach accordingly.

I paused to run through the video I had recorded and picked up on a few clues that I should have noticed before. A couple people had some duplicate elements that were anomalies, like having exactly the same wrist communicator, a shade of hair (despite a different cut), the same model augment visors but different clothing tastes, etc. In these times of forced ultra-consumerism, it was rare that random people had the same models unless they were issued to them that way. Nature did not generate a perfect match of shade/hue/ saturation of color in hair. And so on...

Using those as filters, I started to eliminate duplicates as being false and ended up with nobody. Either there was no meeting, and this was just a test of my responses by Warlock (since he was the only one I knew of capable of this level of illusion), but I doubted that was the case, or there had to be a reason for a physical meet such as a hand off or exchange of some kind. Going back through the feed yet again with ultraviolet/ infra-red enhancements, various zoom angles, and object size comparisons, I got it.

There were 3 of them, and they each had two doubles with articles and features altered that occupied 9 tables. The 10th person was an anomaly, however, as the scans did not show her as human. I froze and very carefully re-ran my analysis and simulation routines. The same result. She was not human. That was out of the question. To my knowledge, none of my kind had EVER succumbed to the delusion of spiritual freedom espoused by these Destabilizers. The reduction in productivity of a regular sheep was bad enough, but the very concept that one of my kind would participate or be in Collaboration with this group was simply unthinkable. There had to be another explanation.

Really, though, I did not have time for this. I had three targets that were likely getting farther and farther away. Smiling slightly, I picked the one with the shortest legs. It did not matter in a modern world with electro-bikes, hyper cars, and jets that could hover and land in the street if needed, but I felt a certain sense of what the sheep called "irony". The chase was on.

Did the sheep know who was coming for them? Was their fear draining them even now? Usually, I could get a sense for this based on their tracks, but the trace here was very faint. I thought that the data void search trick I had used might have caused them to try fading into my normal data flow, but I should have noticed an anomaly of a new insertion into the data mix if that was the case.

Did they have cyber backup spoofing trails for them to blend into? Other sheep, when properly motivated, had told of a hacker with the code name Cipher, but I had never gotten proof of his (or her) existence. That either made them very, very good or a myth. Given my regard for the sheep and their level of conformity to the system over the years, I had dismissed this "Cipher" as a fairy tale the sheep told themselves to help them hold onto hope despite the clear reality of their daily existence. I was especially convinced of my "myth" conclusion by obvious reports of "magic" creatures that aided this hacker and others. Naturally, Warlock, one of the other Molusk Executives and one of the "War Twins," would love to tell me how he convinced the humans of what they needed to think and feel with his version of magic on a daily basis, but that was hardly the same. Just thinking of his smug expression hardened my resolve and bade me dismiss these flights of fancy from my mind.

Of course, I was hard-pressed to keep that resolve when my sensors continued struggling with what should be obvious heat signatures, sound reverberations, and other mechanical evidence of my quarry's passage, and I detected odd frequencies surrounding the trail I followed. Maybe… It did not matter. I had a trail, however faint, and I was going to run this sheep DOWN. She was tricky. Up buildings, around alleys, and even doubling back a couple times at different levels of the mega-building structures, but it seemed like I was getting ever closer even though my progress was much slower than it had ever been against a human target.

I finally cornered her in a city distribution building run by Warlord (one of the War Twins and the one responsible for logistics and strategy), where the automated trucks, trains, and aerial transports maintained the multi-modal infrastructure for the city. With the high complexity level, the facility had a processing capacity that exceeded even my own, and I smiled to myself when her trail led to the hardened storage area for energy cells and other incendiary components that no one wanted to go off and destroy an entire quadrant of the city. She must not have realized there would be no exit there!

Now was the time to strike! No sheep was going to escape me, and there would be no one to hear her cries when this hunt reached its inevitable conclusion. Finally, I could sense residual heat from her passage leading into what she probably thought was a tunnel but was really a bunker designed to fit several train cars together to minimize the unloading and loading of volatile materials in transit that needed to be stored until the next segment of their journey.

I raced in to seal her fate before she realized her situation and returned to the open. As I reached the end of the storage tunnel, however, I sensed that she was not there. No one was. At that moment, I picked up the sonic and mechanical vibrations of the blast doors closing on the entrance. I used all my speed to spring back before it was too late, but I just missed it. As the door closed, I saw that 10th "person" from the meeting on the other side. As the last sliver of light faded, I could just make out the human-looking and intricately formed (but clearly motorized) iris zoom in to lock gazes with me. I felt a shock in that brief moment and felt a part of me reaching out to the other as darkness reaches out to the setting sun. Then the doors closed, and the moment was gone.

No! It was not possible. Unthinkable.

I had to tell the boss. There could be others in our midst helping the enemy! Hmmmm. On second thought, that was not a good idea. What exactly would I tell the boss? How would he react to this catastrophic information on top of my losing to the sheep at the meeting? I knew exactly how it would go. Badly. No, there was only one solution. This evening did not happen.

The record will show that I was pursuing an anomaly (sort of true) and a malfunction of the unpatched AI managing this area of the transport facility, which was simply overloaded and locked me in here until I let myself out. Well, that is what the logs, forensic evidence, and surveillance cameras would show when I was finished with my "adjustments." So, I would live another day.

I had a feeling, though, that what passed for my dreams would no longer be the sweet fear of others that I had been raised to cherish. Things were different, and at some deep level, I knew that <u>I</u> was different. Something that I had always considered to be a secret part of me that made me special had responded to that other.

So many questions. HOW had they fooled my sensors? Was there some mythical hacker on their side? I know that I followed someone or something into that tunnel, but had ample proof that it was empty except for me. Finally, and most distressing, what happened to the non-human that was in the mix. If they could get to one of us, what did that mean for the rest of us? No way I could tell the boss but… For the first time in my existence, I knew I would be facing some night terrors of my very own.

CHAPTER 3

"SEEING IS BELIEVING"

Chapter Synopses: Warlock, One of the War twins (Warlord and Warlock), Street name, Mephistopheles, responsible for overseeing Molusk Corp's businesses that entertain and enthrall the masses. Communications, broadcasting, content curation, hotels, night clubs, and news channels were all part of the bright side of his magical realm. Of course, where there is light, there are shadows. And not all magic is illusion…

It was late Friday night when Cipher and Iris, or The Engineer as she was formally referred to in the Collaborators' listings, met with DJ Gurl to finalize the details for tomorrow's run. They had learned that there was a narrow window of opportunity that Cipher would be able to create alongside a distraction that Iris would be able to orchestrate with some of the catering robots at the event to allow DJ Gurl the chance to enter undetected, set up her equipment, and prep a link for Cipher from the inside. Things had to go smoothly, or they could be in some serious trouble. As Cipher had said, however, they really had no choice.

It turned out that Molusk Corp was throwing a party for key politicians and city leadership Saturday night, and all the A-list members from the city's elite would be in attendance. Cipher had intercepted communication between Molusk Corp Executives, indicating that Warlock (aka Mephistopheles) had a project that was coming out of its stealth mode.

While Warlord was an obvious threat with his direct approach, Warlock was something of an enigma. He was certainly a wiz at communications and broadcasting, but there was more to it than that. Reportedly, his grasp of psychology was uncanny, as was his seeming ability to convince people to **want** what he wanted. Beyond that, there were even stranger rumors, scarcely to be believed. Telekinesis? Teleportation? ESP? These things were hard to credit, but as the Virtual Shaman was teaching them, there were more things in heaven and earth than are dreamt of in the average person's philosophy or something like that. Regardless of the Collaborator's concerns about these rumors, they had a much more immediate problem.

According to the intercepted message, the Executive team led by Warlord and Warlock read that while it would be simpler to force city officials to do what Molusk Corp TOLD them to do with the threat of force, history had shown that, in the long run, parties, bribes, favors (i.e., tools of influence) were a far easier path. That did not mean things could not be made more efficient, however. Warlock planned to test a much more industrial version of his "persuasive broadcasting." It operated like the type used by their fellow executive, N1ght T3rR0r, for use in one-on-one scenarios or with a handful of spectators in relative surprise (did THAT come as a shock to the Destabilizer team when they learned about it!). This version was intended to utterly convince the entire throng to think, act, and vote exactly as Warlock programmed them to. So, naturally, this had to be stopped at a minimum. The stretch goal was to find and eliminate or corrupt the source code behind this new and dangerous tool of the enemy.

Together, they had identified several potential weak points to exploit in the Warlock's operation as well as a necessary sequence of events that they needed to orchestrate in order for the various plan elements to be successful. The challenge would be to convince the master of manipulation to do what THEY needed him to do when it needed to be done, and without suspecting their intent, all on his home ground.

After a series of run-throughs and "what if" testing, they were as ready as they could be; with nothing left to do until the operation commenced, they called it a night and went to get some rest.

At the Event…

Warlock was in his element. As usual, he was projecting a glamour (in actuality, he used a holographic projection-mapped image from near-invisible drones that created whatever effect he wanted, but he liked to refer to his tools in fantastical analogs). With his drones, he could change his shape and dress or even appear to vanish. Between this, the proximity suggestion capabilities he had shared with Nitro, and his innate speed and strength, he had never needed to dig deeper into his bag of tricks. People were easy, crowds, generally so. One did have to be careful to steer mob mentality carefully to avoid losing control of the "group momentum" but as long as he had the key influencers in the crowd, they were little different than any animal herd. They tended to follow their alphas.

The corrupt top of the civic food chain, however, was both a harder and an easier problem to deal with. Their greed made them easy to convince in the early stages of the relationship, but their sheer arrogance and sense of self-importance eventually made them a problem. It was almost like watching a radioactive isotope decay in well-predicted half-life increments. The approach was better than outright war in the streets but so wasteful. Either they became too expensive and had to be "retired," or they were so useless they realized that they had no leverage and had to be "retired." Smiling to himself, he made a mental note of his air quotes and told himself that some of them did actually get to retire with their ill-gotten gains. Some of them.

But no more!!!! Tonight would change that. Tonight, he would forge a new way for Molusk Corp to achieve its corporate and, as a side effect, governmental objectives. He was, naturally, also pleased with HIS additional influence and power to further his private schemes. Very pleased indeed. Things were moving to a phase where broad control of city government, and not just his current level of control via the media, would be necessary.

As the time for "music and speeches" neared, Warlock was going through the plan again in his mind. The initial music would act as a carrier wave for the harmonics he had programmed into the music software. Fixed position projectors (basically larger versions of his personal units) would execute a series of lighting and faint, abstract images that were subtly projected onto all surfaces, including people.

These images, when stared at directly, would appear to be no more than scintillating dots or geometric shapes but, when absorbed by the optic nerves in their totality, be translated by the sub conscious mind. This autostereogram (or Magic Eye) trick as a variation of stenographic encoding had been used for decades to hide information in images, and this was a next-generation concept he had developed himself. The hyper computing needed for large-scale projection maps that made a room full of moving people appear from multiple viewpoints as a flat canvas for reprograming the subconscious mind of the observer while synchronizing with the programing via auditory nerves was demanding but well within the building's AI capabilities.

As an additional preparation, very mild chemical loads in the food and drink would dissolve into special amino acids that opened up specific neural pathways to make the audience more receptive to these stimuli, thus amplifying their efficacy by an order of magnitude.

Satisfied that he had left nothing to chance with the environment, he turned to the speeches.

This was another innovation. Using the boring and pedantic oration to hide the hidden messages was something he was especially proud of. Unlike the music, he was actually programing the voice payload from the speaker to have destructive interference such that the audience was hearing totally different words at the time the sound reached their ears than what the speaker was saying.

All of this was clever, he thought as he gave himself a self-congratulatory pat on the back. Everything was in order, and his security staff was ready to deploy in the event that something, anything really, went wrong. The speakers would read their speeches. Recording media would confirm what they said, but if the crowd was not under his sway and heard HIS message for what it was? So what? There was simply no proof, and HE controlled all the media coverage to make sure it stayed that way. If necessary, he would record their "ravings" and have them submitted to medical treatment where they would emerge as a changed person. It was brilliant!

So, the music was about to start, and the crowd would soon begin to "**clatter.**" There was a loud sound as one of the catering robots went into a seizure. Another one kept trying to take the coat off a young lady who was not currently wearing one. Others simply froze in place, even in mid-stride.

Clearly, this was not a simple malfunction; this was an attack! Unlike a normal human, Warlock split his consciousness into independent processing nodes and instantly operated as multiple internal copies of himself. One node was scanning all communications in and out of the building. Another was isolating visual anomalies from his own optic feed as well as the drones, surveillance, and even private feed from AI goggles, glasses, earpieces, and wrist communication devices. Nothing.

Zooming on the affected robots from multiple angles and magnifications, he spotted the anomaly. He could see that someone had hand-inserted a malware device in the update ports of all the affected units. That meant manually removing and wiping them. He sent a couple of his limited internal personality constructs to piggyback onto stand-by security units to speed up the process, only to find that several of THEM were also victims of this attack.

While parts of his mind coordinated the cleanup, another part sent the physical drive (in the form of a crystal matrix shaped like a spike to fit the custom port, nice work) to an isolated analysis machine in his sanctum. Realizing that he had spread himself too thin, he notified the master of ceremonies that there would be a brief delay but to invite the guests to refresh their food and beverage trays. He was not going to abort his plan yet. This was just a delay, but first, he needed to evaluate the threat.

Remotely operating the robot in his sanctum, he was surprised at the analysis of the drive contents. It appeared that all of this was simply a prank to get his attention. The kid certainly (and the nature of the prank pointed to this being a gifted adolescent) had guts and ability and picked the wrong night to "audition" for his organization. Still, it might be worth an interview. If things went well, then all would be forgiven, and a promising protégé would be discovered. If not, well, he would have many other options to choose from. He would just have to see.

Meanwhile, he had a trial to conduct.

Robots were cleared of the prankish malware, and all his nodes returned to their, his core identity; it was time to give the audience a common goal and a new sense of conviction. A sense of purpose, HIS purpose.

Things kicked off exactly as planned. He could see his sonic routines moving through the software and sense the vibrations caused by destructive interference, reshaping the words of the speakers. As he monitored the audience for that growing sense of collective purpose under his will and thought he saw signs of it working until he noticed that they were giving side glances in his direction. That is to be expected. He did feature as the benevolent mentor in the drama he had scripted, but that was not consistent with the looks he saw. These were angry looks. Worse, these were very alert looks. Someone had tampered with the chemical cocktails administered by the catering robots that should have rendered the audience pliant and suggestible.

Quickly, he sent several of his drones to be proximal to the ears of several guests to pick up on the modified speech they were hearing and was outraged! Rather than the sense of purpose and obedience he should be hearing, he was hearing his own plans laid plain for the listener to hear.

He immediately attempted to modify the programming to combat this attack. Yes, it turns out that it WAS an attack after all. A double-blind that had totally fooled him. The insult would be addressed later. For now, he was frustrated, although not terribly surprised at this point, to find that he was locked out of a number of his in-house systems. He could get through, of course; he was simply too good once he focused his energy and will on the problem, but he also had a growing physical threat to contend with first.

Several important guests had brought their own security teams with them and were sending several his way to detain him or hold him to task for what they heard. He was not sure what their intentions were, but he did not care to accept them passively. He was not a sheep. He could have simply disappeared using his personal holographic capabilities, but he had a better idea. Humans always said that "Seeing was believing." Well, his "believing" experiment was shot so he needed to be working on the "seeing" part.

First, he broadcast on all channels out of the building. Some of those appeared to have been shut down, but his empire was communication, and he had too many systems with a wide range of access controls to block him entirely, and some got out. Good! He notified all channels and agencies that he could reach that he was a victim of a corporate attack by competitors of Molusk Corp.

He just hoped that this would help confuse the audience and outside parties and shock their aggression with some FUD (Fear, Uncertainty, and Doubt). Then he started running for the open doors to the balcony.

Since they were on the 78th floor, he was certain no one would try to get in his way. This was critical to his plans. He had the room projection units cloak him so he was invisible; at the same time, he had his personal drones continue to project the image of him running and jumping out of the window. Even though they had not been chemically affected, the visual preparations had to have SOME effect, and when the human mind was weakened and faced with visual inconsistencies, it was much easier to sow further confusion. What had they heard, really? Could they trust that memory if their eyes had so clearly been confused? Was Warlock just a victim? Well, it was a starting point.

Knowing that he was clear of the audience's focus, he casually walked to the side of the room, invisible, as the audience gasped at his apparent suicide. Chuckling silently, he had the drones change his image to that of a phoenix that soared up into the night in a fiery streak. With any luck, he could spin most of this drama into a publicity stunt gone awry.

When everyone had left, still talking about what had transpired with increasingly inaccurate clarity, he returned to visible condition and went to retrieve the spike of his programming. It was not there. Concerned, he raced back to the main processing unit to check and, again, not really surprised, to find that the very robot that he had sent through all his safeguards to the isolated testing unit had been further modified and, while he was distracted in the ballroom, had inserted a REAL malicious code stream that corrupted the centralized source code as well as multiple variants all the way back to isolated code strands that bore little resemblance to the version he was to test tonight.

He was back to square one, but it was only a setback. In the meantime, he had a "prankster" to track down. He had a whole arsenal that they were unaware of that he was now willing to bring to play. His time of playing in the shadows was coming to an end. Seeing was believing indeed, he doubted that they would believe the reality of what he would soon bring into play, but their belief was not required. Warlock was coming! To give them a taste of his control over quantum energy, he made sure that the spike that was stolen was still entangled with his storage units and sent the wipe command to all units in the entangled grouping. There was nowhere the assailant could hide, no distance they could travel, no protection they could erect, short of a quantum standing wave of their own, that could stop the wipe. They have literally stolen NOTHING.

The team met briefly before they dispersed. They learned long ago that centralized behaviors were vulnerable, and they were definitely going to be the object of Molusk Corp search teams and even private bounty hunters. Nothing new there. Despite the VERY successful run, there was tension in the air. When Iris' compromised robot had passed along the physical spike now holding the contents of Warlock's private data files, and Cipher had tried to crack the encryption, he had encountered serious quantum-level protection. He had managed to get past the first layer to the header record before he saw a self-destruct command emerge from nowhere into the spike that wiped the spike clean. In the brief moments that he had, he copied the data to his own isolated rig. Good move as clearly the Warlock had somehow enabled a passive quantum entanglement field that deleted the bits on his disconnected drive at the same time the corresponding bit was deleted from Warlock's file. That was new.

Writing down what he could still recall in case his own memory might somehow be at risk, heck, this was still new tech, he sat back and scratched his head. It seemed like there was a whole list of projects that Warlock had been working on, and this was just one of them. Well, that was a worry for another day. Tonight, they would take the win, and the city could go back to business as usual and choose what THEY wanted vs what a central authority told them they wanted. It was a good day.

CHAPTER 4

"ALL WAR IS DECEPTION"

© SYNTHTOPIA #0923:

Chapter Synopses: Warlord, One of the War twins (Warlord and Warlock), Street name, Agamemnon, responsible for overseeing business "on the street" for Molusk Corp. Freight, construction, transport, garbage, manufacturing, he makes sure everything runs smoothly. If something caused a problem, well, they found out what a ten-ton truck really feels like.

Warlord stood entranced by the beauty of his "empire" as it was projected onto a three-dimensional display. Air, land, and sea transports moved around the various regions in a flawless choreography that was simply awe-inspiring. Billions of tons of materials and countless personnel moved from one point to another, weaving in and out of air channels, threading across maglev rail cross-connects, and speeding on massive hydrofoils to make their payloads seem like they weighed nothing at all.

THIS was POWER, he thought. Not for him the influence, illusions, and appearances that his brother, Warlock, favored. No. His was pure, simple power. Power to move what he needed to where it needed to be. Power to extract the maximum value and beyond from such movement and, importantly, power to remove any and all obstacles that stood in his way.

The hidden counterpoint to all this efficiency was that, yes, he got things where they were needed when they were needed to produce the maximum profitability. As a "public service," his transport business was impartial. What a concept. Of course, getting Molusk goods to market faster than the competition but not in such an obvious way to give the authorities a reason to interfere was the TRUE optimization. He was a Master.

Even more masterful was the benefit of being the orchestration layer for moving goods and services. Market values for commodities were reactive in nature. He could create a "sandwich attack" where commodities in transit via a tank transport could be sequenced such that their arrival earlier or later in a convoy had a subtle shift to the availability for orders in the market. This in turn, would have small changes to market prices that he could predict and arbitrage under a different corporate entity, of course. All of this while still technically delivering "within negotiated parameters." That was true mastery, even more so when no one noticed.

As his nom de guerre suggested, he was far more than just an operations and efficiency-focused being. He was a general in his own right with a deep discipline in all aspects of marshal history and precedent. Machiavelli, Musashi, von Clausewitz, and Sun Tzu were just a small sampling of his favorite historical figures, but they were as much a part of his personality construct as they were central to his many plans, within plans, within plans. The beautiful complexity and flawless execution that was a hallmark of his visible operations were also embedded in his non-visible operations. After all, "All war is deception," and BUSINESS was WAR!

Strength from Weakness

Just as the various transports were his troops, energy plants, his food supplies, goods for sale, and his ammunition, he also had "spies". Many of these were digital constructs or AIs, some were robotic, and a few were even human. Through these agents, he managed an entirely different dance featuring illicit goods, pilfered equipment, and, where needed, sabotage of competing central marketplaces.

One agent might swap out the contents of two legal component containers, resulting in a delivery where each ended up rejected. Since return process flows were inherently less optimized than delivery systems, the originator would often opt for destination (local) liquidation rather than pay for return transport and re-integration into the supply chain. Since he caused the issue in the first place, Warlock's agents were always in the right place, at the right time to bid on the "bad deliveries" and flip them rapidly to prearranged local buyers for a tidy profit. The best part for him was that the competition ended up paying for the delivery of what became his goods to his customers.

Alternatively, illegal chemicals could be placed in the same container from a rival marketplace and delivered to yet ANOTHER marketplace while also reporting a "concern" to authorities. This would result in both sender and receiver being implicated in illicit trafficking. Another well-placed tip would ensure that the media shared the story widely (his brother was quite good at this particular angle), and consumer confidence (and spending) would dip, at least for a while. If things went very well, that spending would shift to his marketplace, and he would receive a windfall on both sides of that event.

While the accumulation of seemingly small errors meant that it appeared he was less than perfect in his domain of operations, the reality was that NOTHING was ever out of place in his world. Well, at least not for long. Meanwhile, profits flowed, and the dance continued.

The Discipline of the Army

One day, Warlord received a sealed, encrypted offline message to his street name "Agamemnon." His agents were using a new quantum encryption seal to prevent tampering. Only he had the private keys capable of unlocking the message once it was sealed, even though any of his agents could seal a message with their own unique key codes. His brother had developed that one, and it was coming in very handy since the competition and authorities were always a potential concern.

The irony was not lost on him that his brother was taking a page from the Destabilizer playbook (without really buying into that whole decentralization nonsense, of course). After he was debriefed on the events of the attack on the public event his brother was planning on using to control city leaders, he was even more vigilant than ever.

Imagine an anonymous attacker using the <u>same</u> <u>method</u> Warlock had planned to use to control the sheep being turned around and used against him by actually informing them of his brother's plans. Not to mention getting him to walk them right into his heavily guarded sanctum to destroy the source codes of his work! This displayed a disturbing amount of inside information, coordination, diverse skill sets, and advanced planning. Well, his brother could be a little too reliant on his gadgets and illusions and forget that the path to victory came from clean strategy and discipline. He sighed. Perhaps his brother would learn from HIS example.

So, opening the message and scanning it as well as authenticating the sender and contents for data gaps or misdirection, he was satisfied as to its authenticity, if not with the message itself. He had a double agent. Unacceptable.

It appeared that one of his agents had accepted an offer to place illegal substances in a package that was supposed to contain ultra-pure R.A.M. chips from the latest generation and place a trojan horse inside the original shipping crate. It was not an accident, as his own plans had been to swap this particular payload out in one of his ongoing shell games. This one WAS different in that the R.A.M. was officially en route to his own marketplace, and the swap was, in actuality, an elaborate insurance fraud scheme. The plan was clever but a little disturbing. It displayed a familiarity with his operations that this agent should not have had. Was there *another* double agent in his organization?

The weakest links were, usually, the human employees, but he could not rule out a subversion of obedience routines among his AIs. Several were of a high enough order that they could be bribed with extra access to data sets, processing power, or even physical assets these days. Such things had been possible since the tokenization of real-world assets and machine-to-machine commerce was enabled with currencies that ran on trustless servers. He always hated that, however, as it basically validated the Destabilizer credo, but he had to admit, it worked. The massive lift in productivity that such structures delivered was simply too much to ignore or stifle, so these systems were allowed to persist.

Assuming that such an agent existed, he held all the control of his direct systems, so none of the agents should have been able to gain access to this information. Warlord decided that he needed more intelligence. He would need to root out the traitor, extract the information he required, and make an example of him, her, or it. A very clear and permanent example.

In the meantime, he decided to turn this bit of misfortune into a tactical advantage. First, he swapped the manifests such that the original R.A.M. would be intercepted early by unrelated agents of his and shipped to a secure location for his retrieval. Then, he arranged for the original R.A.M. to be replaced with defective assets in the original R.A.M. packaging with encoded tags identifying them as the original. If it were not for his access to central systems, he would not have been able to circumvent that specific safeguard. The benefits of being in charge of enforcing the rules, he thought as he smiled to himself.

Finally, he re-routed the swapped-out R.A.M. order to go to a competitor so he could tip the police about the theft of his container and claim the inferior product had been planted there by the innocent competition (innocent? Hardly). Finally, the illicit package was routed to yet ANOTHER enemy for a similar raid by authorities with full press coverage, courtesy of his brother. Overall, it is a beautiful and efficient strategy.

After that plan was executed and the new one brought to fruition, he planned on devoting his full attention to cleaning the house. A **deep** cleaning.

Cutting the Swallow

Warlord and his trusted agents moved swiftly. His long years of practicing flawless execution of multilayered strategy were put to the test. He was not quite relieved when all the swaps had been executed, the competition had made **their** swaps, and he could move on to the secure location to retrieve the R.A.M. for his special project (which happened to need this particular and untraceable R.A.M. for its next phase and not even Molusk was to be aware of it).

As he arrived at the drop location, he tuned in to monitor the raids in real time and ensure his brother's agents spread the word as they had agreed before the exercise. It did not take long to realize that something was horribly wrong. The container that was supposed to hold illicit drugs and that the manifest showed they were the rightful owner of the new R.A.M. It actually held the new R.A.M.!!!! HIS R.A.M. Meanwhile, the container that was supposed to show defective R.A.M. with his certified labels showed nothing but a scrap delivery both in the container and on the manifest. At that moment, he heard the sound of heavy military vehicles, the mechanized police, arriving to surround him. He did not need to retrieve and open the container; he knew he would be here to know that the illicit drugs he intended for others would be in it. He was in trouble.

Leave no enemy alive behind you

Well, he would have been in trouble if he had not been who he was. Again, Warlord was not an affectation. Yes, he had legendary skills in tactics and coordination, but the power of his central authority was daunting in its own right. He rapidly scanned local grid traffic for all transports and spotted a couple candidates. He was actually very lucky! Working quickly, if not frantically, slow was smooth, and smooth was FAST in these things; he set his impromptu plans in motion.

As the enforcement units arrived and search bots were deployed to scan the area for the contraband they had been informed would be here, three things occurred nearly simultaneously.

A heavily armored energy transport carrying volatile material destined for the local power station went off course and rammed into the enforcement unit ranks in the midst of their deployment. This halted the search units as the nature of the invading vehicle became known, and they started to search it for hijackers or leakage.

Secondly, a low-flying transport drone used for package transport to residential units swooped low enough for Warlord to jump up and be caught in the drone's delivery claw and whisk him outside of the immediate zone.

Third, just as the enforcement units on the periphery were becoming aware of Warlord's exit, a high-speed, automated courier jet slammed into the ground, right on top of the energy transport. The resulting fireball was nothing short of impressive.

Further, the "accidental" EMP blast fried any circuits in the enforcement units that had survived the physical damage from heat and kinetic energy of the blast. Not only was there no record of his presence, but all traces of whatever was in the package waiting for him were destroyed as well.

Warlord was angry. It had been a long, long time since he had been outmaneuvered. Worse, he had been outmaneuvered with his own strategies WHILE he was playing his own game. Something was definitely wrong. His agent, the one linked in the message, had known nothing. Worse, it looked like he was not really involved at all, which meant he had been tricked further into eliminating yet another asset from the board and by a message delivery system that should have been foolproof.

To add insult to injury, he had to audit all of his systems for the authorities in order to assist in their investigation of the strange triple failure of various transport units that had resulted in the unfortunate loss of an entire enforcement squad. He was able to mitigate the reputational damage somewhat by implying that it was the Destabilizer group and their Collaborators, even though everyone knew that this was not their style. His brother Warlock cooperated since his news leads were flops, and he needed some cover as well. Limited effectiveness as a tactical move, but it managed to muddy the waters a bit.

Meanwhile, his profit was down, he had lost assets, and his personal project was behind schedule. He would need to meet with his brother Warlock and their peer, N1ght T3rR0r, and formulate a plan that had them work together. Someone was beating them using their own tools and tactics. He intended their victory to just be for the battle and not the war.

War was, after all, HIS domain!

CHAPTER 5

"ALL HANDS ON DECK"

© SYNTHTOPIA #0089

Chapter Synopses: Warlock's Command Ship, the "SS Enchantment" Stealth, broadcast, and offensive capabilities make it a watery home away from home. The Executive Team is holding an "All hands on deck" meeting to strategize over the disruption in operations. Everything is definitely NOT smooth sailing!

The "SS Enchantment" was more than just a ship—it was a monolithic testament to Warlock's power and stature. The ship, with its aggressive angles and sharp contours, sat ominously against the amber backdrop of the night sky. Neon lights along its body gave it an ethereal glow, making it seem as though the ship was alive. Its presence commanded respect, and to be aboard it was a privilege that only a few had earned.

Of course, the Warlock was a master of illusion, and the ship had a full array of the Warlock's favorite tools. It could shimmer and disappear with optical camouflage or even look like a different vessel altogether. The broadcast emitters would change registry identification (illegal of course but useful) and also keep both automated and manually steered craft away. Approaching vessel GPS carrier signals were subtly modified to misdirect the automated vessels while sonic vibrations below the audible range carried easily over the wavetops to create an aversion field few people would be able to overcome.

Within its opulent chambers, Warlock, Warlord, and Nitro convened. The room was a meld of advanced technology and opulent luxury. Screens displayed data streams while plush seating provided comfort to the trio. Comfort was one function of the room, naturally, but it, like the ship, was designed to make a statement. That statement was POWER. Of course, all three of them were technically peers so they were theoretically on a level playing field. This meeting was important, but an Executive always needs to be ready to seize an advantage wherever possible. No exceptions. Not in the Molusk culture.

Nitro, always one for dramatics, entered last, his cloak trailing behind him. "Warlock, Warlord," he greeted with a nod. Unable to resist, Warlord responded with a smirk, "You are late. Do take a seat; you look tired, and your energy seems…off." That last part was unscripted. While he had meant it as part of their usual power games, Nitro did indeed seem tired. Not only that, there *was* something off in his energy scans that gave Warlord pause. Was Nitro slipping? Nitro did not respond.

Warlock, not one to waste time, gestured for them all to be seated. "We've been outmaneuvered, gentlemen, using our own techniques. This isn't the work of amateurs or the ill-informed. Their ability to adapt our own technology against us in ways we do not understand and coordinate psychological, cyber, robotic, and physical attacks with the degree of skill displayed so far speaks to significant resources and insights."

Warlord grunted in agreement; his eyes shadowed. "They've eluded my best sentinels." This drew a smirk from Nitro that he ignored. He continued, "Systems analysis and transport record searches show no anomalies. Whoever they are, they're well-trained and able to move through my physical systems as easily as they move through your surveillance..." he looks at Nitro, less for a dig but rather in shared disbelief, and finishes, "Without a trace!"

That last part hit Nitro harder than Warlord knew. Nitro was still haunted by the impossible escape from his quarry in the storage tunnel, but neither of his peers had those details, not after he erased the evidence. Still, Warlord could tell that something was missing from Nitro's tampering, while none of them could determine what or how the enemy did what they did.

Nitro leaned forward, steepling his fingers. "The question is, who would dare oppose us? We've crushed all significant threats. We can assume the Destabilizers and their allies are part of this, but they have always been focused on helping people and "spiritual development" or such nonsense. Nothing overtly directed our way. My own organization has not had any serious challenges or setbacks until recent events. Yes, there have been hints and rumors of people with special abilities or mystic allies– but as you are both aware but none of them have ever been confirmed. Mysteries. Miracles. Magic. These are things that the sheep accept, NOT US!!!" He slammed his palm down on the table. Normally such an outburst would have been picked at as a weakness, but they all shared his frustration.

The room was silent for a moment, the gravity of their situation palpable.

Warlock's voice cut through, "It doesn't matter who they are, but what they know. Knowledge is power, and right now, they have the upper hand in that area. Knowledge of our operations, techniques, capabilities, and at least <u>some</u> of our secrets..." he paused to look at Warlord before continuing, "...place us in an untenable position. It will not be long before this rises to the attention of Tyrannus!" They all knew what that implied. No one felt the need to comment on that warning any further.

Nitro sighed. "We need information, and we need it fast."

Warlock and Nitro turned their eyes to Warlord, the master strategist. "You are both correct. We played our hands and lost the round, but, we have a wildcard," he said with a sly smile.

"The Demon," Warlock whispered, a hint of both admiration and anxiety coloring in his tone.

Warlord nodded. "Exactly. She's our best chance at uncovering this shadowy force. Who else has delivered with her track record when we have come to a standstill in the past? She has greater latitude and, how shall we say, plausible deniability. After all, she is not, technically, a corp employee." He looked at Nitro, knowing he would object. The Demon's methods and domain overlapped his considerably, and he never liked it when they had to use her. There also seemed to be a deep seeded dislike between them that went far beyond professional rivalry. The War Twins had both seen it and took advantage of every chance to interfere with Nitro's autonomy.

Nitro grumbled, "She's reckless. A double-edged sword." He almost said more but knew this was his problem, and to lay it out would only give his rivals an even greater edge to use against him.

"But she's effective," Warlord countered. "She's infiltrated places we thought impenetrable and found the information we thought lost forever, or at least too well-hidden to recover. If anyone can uncover this enemy, it's her."

Nitro pondered for a moment, then nodded. "Very well. We will task The Demon with this mission. But let's be clear: she is to gather information only.

No unsanctioned strikes, and she stays on a tight leash." In the back of his mind, he was thinking of the old saying, never raise more devils than you can put down. He hoped that they would be up to the task here with a demon. He *knew* that they could not trust The Demon. Not that he felt any trust with these two, but is always seemed to be "just business" with their behaviors. The Demon felt different. She seemed to treat ruthlessness and betrayal as virtues in their own right.

After a moment, all three men nodded in agreement.

As the meeting concluded, Warlock stood up, looking out of the large panoramic window. The reflections of the city lights played across the water, their shimmering dance interrupted only by the looming shadow of the "SS Enchantment."

"We'll come out of this on top," he declared with more confidence, perhaps, than he felt. "We always do."

The trio dispersed, each carrying the weight of the coming storm. The next moves would be critical, and the fate of their corporate empire hinged on the intelligence The Demon would bring. Only time would tell if they could overcome the unseen adversary that dared to challenge them.

CHAPTER 6

"COLLABORATORS ASSEMBLE"

© SYNTHTOPIA #1633

Chapter Synopses: Collaborators come together at the cybernetic round table to share information and plan their next moves. Are they solving a puzzle? Or discovering a new one?

The dimly lit room was filled with an electric tension. At its heart, a table bristling with holographic displays, streams of data, and the unmistakable hum of groundbreaking technology. Around this table, seven individuals—each a force to be reckoned with—came together. DJ Gurl, Iris (The Engineer), Daedalus (The Inventor), Eve, Cipher (The Hacker), Artemis (Moon Maiden), and Cyber Bill, collectively known as part of the Zenith group or more commonly "the Collaborators," united against a shared enemy. In the holographic display, the Spirit Animal "The Electron Cat" MEO was in attendance to run cybercall on the meeting and prevent electronic eavesdropping.

Eve, with her artificial, piercing eyes, broke the silence. "We each bring pieces to this puzzle. Let's see if we can create a full picture that will make some sense of them."

Cipher, ever the authority on all things in cyberspace, cleared his throat, "Nitro's use of AI surveillance is unprecedented. His tactics aren't just about traditional spying; he's using AI programs designed specifically to target individuals, to identify gaps created by our cloaking techniques, to hack into private data lakes and government repositories alike, and he has an uncanny ability to adapt his intrusion programs on the fly." Pausing for a moment, Cipher added, looking apologetically towards MEO's image, "I've found that our Spirit Animal allies unintentionally made it easier for these programs to track us on the last mission even though it was their abilities that enabled us to spoof his systems in the first place as well as execute our trap for Nitro thanks to Shadow's abilities with Space. We will need to make some adaptations of our own to prevent Molusk from isolating and discovering their secrets."

A murmur spread across the table. Iris, the tech genius, piped up, "That means we need to enhance our digital disguises, or better yet, develop countermeasures against Nitro's surveillance that do not rely on those abilities until we are sure that they are untraceable. They are our only real edge in this fight, and we cannot risk knowledge of the spirit network or our allies getting out."

She continued with a tone of anxiety, "Yes, Shadow's special abilities allowed Eve to lead Nitro into that trap as well as positioning DJ Gurl and I to interface with Warlock's security, access air-gapped systems to modify programming, and swap out the chemicals used in the food. Even our ability to bypass Warlord's controls of the transportation system relies on that edge."

Cipher's expression said that he did not totally agree with her statement, but he did not argue with her. Still, he needed to talk to her later. Something about her logic seemed to rest more on her recent fascination with understanding the spirit realm than with any real defeatist sentiment. He completely understood wanting to increase knowledge, but she had been working more on networks of the spiritual energy, ancient "lay lines," entities of spirit, expanded consciousness, and how biosynths like Eve and empowered people like Lady Fortuna connected with this energy. Great work, but she needed to stay with their current focus, as did he. He shifted his attention back to the group.

Eve, her tone soft but with a clear edge of steel, recounted her recent encounter with Nitro and noted, "I had a strange moment during my run-in with Nitro. I managed to trap him in the storage area as planned, but..." She hesitated, a hint of vulnerability in her voice. "There's... a connection between us. I felt it then; I feel it now! It feels achingly familiar, and I could sense a change beginning in him… but that doesn't mean we can trust him. Not yet."

DJ Gurl interjected with the rhythm of someone used to the beats of both music and battle, "Warlock's game is one of illusions. He bends the minds of his targets with his auditory and visual influences. Thanks to the tools Iris and our allies have provided, we've had some success against his robotic forces, but we must be wary of his mind games. His city-wide broadcasts are still affecting the people of the city, and his control of the media has mostly neutralized the negative buzz of gossip after our operation at his gala event. We managed to stop him but not hurt him. My raves are still needed to give the people some measure of resistance and hope, but we need to find a way to increase OUR influence, or all our efforts will be no more than a holding action."

Artemis, always alert to the undercurrents of the city and the gossip of the prominent figures, shared her observations. "The city's elites are in disarray. They might not recall what Warlock did, but there's a palpable disdain for him and his enterprises. It is fading, as Digi (DJ Gurl) described, but that could still be useful to us for a time. If possible, we need to move faster."

Cyber Bill adjusted his glasses and spoke up, "And then there's Warlord. His deceptive tactics are all about amassing wealth in secret via incremental steps and the manipulation of resources and assets of all kinds. I've been digging, and I've discovered that there are secret projects being helmed by both Warlord and Warlock—things they want to remain hidden. Most curious, they appear to be hiding them from Molusk Corp as well!"

Daedalus (Dad), the oldest and wisest of the group and known as The Inventor (and Iris' father), added gravely, "Bill is quite correct. Based on the information we have been able to piece together from our recent activities, it seems Warlock has been working on a novel Quantum Emitter, or QE, designed to power highly advanced quantum effects while Warlord pours resources into a covert lab named Tartarus. We need to find out more."

He continued, "The theoretical potential of the QE is unknown, but it could exceed any weapon we have ever contemplated. Warlock's ability to erase the data we stole from him even after we had it in our possession would be a trivial parlor trick compared to the potential of this emitter. Rather than destroying a building, for example, what about removing it from existence? I must postulate that it could even project destruction through time as well as space. That last is purely theoretical, and I have no idea how they would get the needed power inputs with current technology, but it needs to be on our threat dashboard!"

He took a deep breath and continued, "That makes me even more concerned about what Warlord is up to since they were not satisfied with just the QE. Lastly,

The War Twins have always been at odds with each other forever. If they are working together in secret like this, it means Tyrannus is likely not aware of it. If they slip his leash, I shudder to think of the implications."

The room fell silent, each member absorbing the gravity of the situation. Eve spoke up, "On further contemplation, I do think that we have one ray of hope—Nitro might be redeemable. But we need to tread cautiously, or his years of conditioning will make it impossible. His help, though, would make it worth the risk,"

As the meeting concluded, the Collaborators went their separate ways, their minds heavy with the tasks ahead. Each knew they had to act swiftly, not just for their own sakes but for the city they had sworn to protect.

CHAPTER 7

"DEMONIC POSSESSION"

© SYNTHTOPIA #1608

Chapter Synopses: The Demon (No street name) is Touched by the Terror's Dark energy and is a covert agent of the Executive Team of N1ght T3Rr0r, Warlock and Warlord, but does she have her own agenda?

Amid the neon haze of the cybernetic city, a menacing figure stood tall and imperious. The Demon, with her fierce metallic armor that seemed to come alive in the glow, had commenced her hunt for the Collaborators. She loved having a focus. For a being like her, sitting around talking about corporate projects, operational efficiencies, research initiatives, and the bottom line were pointless. She craved the Wild Hunt as if she was one of the Fey from old. Well, that and the occasional betrayal. She smiled knowingly. It would come soon enough, as Nitro would discover.

No one knew what she looked like, and even fewer knew of her past. She had been a most gifted mercenary turned bounty hunter. She seemed to have a well of energy that drove her on when others quit and an uncanny intuition for the Hunt. She *always* found her target. She had discovered an even greater capacity for deceit and betrayal than she had imagined possible and used it with pleasure.

One such hunt had brought her into contact with her opposite. She had come to learn about her being Touched by the Terror and never considered the energy within her to be anything other than an asset. When she laid her hands on her Light "twin," their whole world changed. Part of her wanted the change, which represented a peace she had never known, while the other part knew she would stop being the Hunter she saw herself as.

Ultimately, she betrayed *herself*, the ultimate victory, and destroyed her target, and almost herself along with him, by triggering an energy overload in their vehicle and diving out to safety, sort of. The blast was both faster and more violent than she had anticipated, and much of her form was scarred as a result. She used augments and what medical miracles she could get and became faster and stronger than ever, but the cosmetic damage was permanent. The person she was had died, and The Demon was born.

When she first met Nitro (the street name for N1ght T3Rr0r), she knew that he was also Touched by the Dark but that he had not yet passed *his* test. He played at being ruthless and fierce, but she saw that it was as much a mask as the one she donned to face the world. In her eyes, he was "unworthy" of his success.

Partly fed by her own bitterness at his position and what she considered to be unfounded arrogance that he was a top hunter in the city, she waited for any chance to take him down a peg. Someday, she thought, she would arrange a more permanent "demotion" for him and take her place on the Executive Team.

Until then, she was on The Hunt!!!

Every contact in the corporate, industrial, and business world knew of The Demon's reputation. Simply put, she was a force that wouldn't hesitate to dismantle anyone in her path. Whispers of her return echoed through boardrooms and back alleys alike, sending shivers down the spines of the most seasoned businessmen and street hustlers. She had been a myth. A legend. The ultimate power broker behind the scenes. And now, she was once again very much real and active on her Hunt.

However, The Demon was too shrewd to soil her hands directly beyond closed doors or in the light of day. There, in private, her strategy was clear: to leverage her vast network and intimidate her contacts into submission. Her contacts would often find themselves cornered in plush offices, locked in face-to-face meetings with The Demon, her piercing helmet optics seeming to bore right into their souls. With each interaction, her intent was made clear: Assist in her Hunt or face dire and immediate consequences.

For the street-level work, she had the perfect asset: Banshee. On the surface, Banshee appeared to be one of Nitro's trusted lieutenants, but in the dark underbelly of the city, everyone knew the truth—Banshee was The Demon's puppet. The Demon smiled; it was an open secret, one that Nitro chose to ignore, believing in his overconfidence that he had the upper hand. The Demon thought otherwise and took great pleasure in her open interference in his organization.

Banshee, with her superlative tracking abilities and network among the street organizations, began her own hunt. She was tasked not only to gather intel but also to marshal The Demon's vast resources of bounty hunters. Each hunter, equipped with the latest tech and driven by the promise of a hefty reward, scoured every nook and cranny of the city. Banshee liked to refer to them as her "wolf pack," but The Demon considered them to be more like jackals. Whatever. As long as they got results, they could consider themselves to be a pride of lions for all she cared.

While The Demon plotted from her high-rise, Banshee was her eyes and ears on the ground. From dusty bars to the slickest nightclubs, she whispered, threatened, and coerced, gathering bits of information. Every lead and every rumor about the Collaborators was meticulously documented and reported back.

As the days turned into nights and the neon lights of the city never dimmed, one thing became abundantly clear to her: The Demon's net was closing in on the Collaborators. The city that once seemed vast and endless to her prey should now feel like a tightening cage. For now, they still seemed to evade almost certain capture or discovery, but The Demon was confident that her methodical approach would leave no stone unturned and nowhere for them to hide.

Throughout it all, Nitro remained, to all appearances, blissfully unaware of the real relationship between The Demon and Banshee. In his arrogance, The Demon thought, he believed he was playing a game, moving pieces on a chessboard as one of the Executive Team. She smiled. Little did he know, he was but a pawn in The Demon's grand design. Yes, betrayal would come soon enough.

CHAPTER 8

"DEATH MAY RIDE A PALE HORSE, BUT I RIDE 800 HORSES"

© SYNTHTOPIA #0407

Chapter Synopses: Banshee's car, a powerful beast designed for running down targets for the Corp. A mix of old-school power and modern tracking gear, Banshee takes great pride in her ride, but can it run down her next target?

Banshee, also known by her clandestine alias 'Syren,' was in no mood for games. She had been scouring the dark alleys and neon-lit streets for days, and every lead seemed to lead to a dead end. "I'm not some damn detective," she muttered to herself, frustrated with the lack of progress. Yes, it felt like their net was closing in on the Collaborators, but time and time again, a certain lead or capture failed.

It was as if they were only seeing part of the picture and that there was a whole different part of the city they could not access. Of course, she refused to believe some of the rumors that had been extracted from their information sources. "Extracted" because after it was initially volunteered, she simply had to put several of their less critical informants under strenuous and sometimes vigorous interrogation.

"What did they expect?" she mused to herself aloud. "When you report seeing a cat that could walk through walls, a tiger fly and disappear, or a regular man with the abilities of a synth because he meditated, you know that you better have proof. Idiots." Well, some of them will recover but what a waste, and still no proof. Whenever they tried to check out the stories with the ever-present surveillance systems, there was nothing. Perhaps, she thought, it was something in Warlock's domain. This was the sort of thing he would get a kick out of doing. His tricks were all illusions, though. He smiled a little too broadly these days whenever anyone implied that. A mystery for another day.

As she stood in deep thought, her car, a sleek beast of metal and neon, idled quietly beside her, humming softly with the power of its 800 horses beneath the hood. Around them, the rain cast a shimmering reflection of the neon city lights onto its surface, making it look even more otherworldly.

Just as Banshee was about to call it a night, an odd sensation prickled the back of her neck. It wasn't something she saw but rather something she didn't see. A void, a brief ripple in the air, as if reality itself was being distorted under the barrage of raindrops, and it was moving away from her. Rapidly!

Without a second thought, Banshee jumped into her ride, its engine roaring to life in an instant. She slammed the accelerator, and the car lunged forward, shooting out like a bullet from a gun. She could sense the distortion moving, apparently fleeing from her, and she was on its tail. Almost literally, she thought, as the distortion seemed to have an outline of a giant feline. This was the break they needed. If she could catch this shadow, they might be able to make sense of how their enemy continued to evade them.

The chase was on.

Banshee's car wove in and out of traffic, its tires screeching against the wet asphalt. The blur of neon signs, holograms, and city lights melded into a single streak as she pursued her nearly unseen quarry. Every ounce of her being was focused on the chase, her instincts sharpened to a razor's edge. Despite the instruments in her car telling her nothing was there, she was not fooled. She was locked on and was not about to let go.

People, cars, and bikes all got out of her way. She had turned on the siren (and if one more person compared it to her name, she was going to make an example of them) that alerted everyone that she was on the chase, and if they did not move, that was their problem. Her car's graphene armor was more than enough to handle minor collisions without leaving a mark on the car.

At one point in the chase, something shut down her on-board comp systems. Perhaps that would have slowed her down if she had a fully digital or automated car, but her ride was old school. Her high-speed chase was on manual, using her advanced reflexes rather than robotic systems that would fail in such an event. The chase continued.

But as she rounded a corner at breakneck speed, a realization dawned on her. Her quarry wasn't just fast; it could apparently fly. The shadowy, catlike figure, surrounded by the telltale shimmer of a distortion field, rose into the air, escaping the confines of the street. For just a moment, Banshee thought she could see a majestic tiger through the haze. There was no sound of wings, blades, jets, or other propulsion systems, but there it was. Whatever it was disappeared as quietly as death riding his pale horse.

"No!" Banshee yelled, pushing her car to its limits. But for all its power, for all its 800 horses, her car was bound to the ground. She skidded to a stop, watching helplessly as the ethereal figure disappeared into the night sky.

She sat there for a moment, the engine's rumble the only sound in the stillness of the night. The message was clear: She might have the mightiest ride on the streets, but this city held secrets beyond her comprehension. She hoped, she sincerely hoped, that this was just a clever illusion like that employed by The Warlock. If their quarry could just...fly...well, she was not sure how they could adapt their procedures to easily counter it. This would take some thought. In the meantime, she was certainly *not* going to be telling anyone about what she thought she saw or her failure. She had no desire for The Demon to "verify" her story. Tomorrow would be another day.

With a heavy sigh, Banshee revved her engine once more, the roar echoing through the empty streets. "Death may ride a pale horse," she whispered to herself, "but this isn't over." And with that, she drove off into the neon night, determined to uncover the mystery that had presented itself this evening.

CHAPTER 9

"AN OUNCE OF PREVENTION..."

Chapter Synopses: The Inventor. Street Name, Daedalus (Dad). Does a machine have a consciousness? A spirit? Can a synthesis between organic and machine have more than an identity? Can it connect beyond its own digital and genetic programming? Can it have a soul? Daedalus is convinced that this is the case. It is all in the design....now if only a synth would come to BELIEVE.

Amidst a myriad of screens, cables, and machines humming with life, Daedalus, or "Dad" as he was affectionately known among the Collaborators, gazed intently at the figure lying on his examination table. Eve, the most sophisticated Synth (Biosynth, he corrected himself) he had ever encountered, lay there with closed eyes. Monitors attached to her lit up with intricate patterns of data, reflecting her unique blend of digital and organic components. As always, he marveled at the implications inherent in her very existence.

As a young man, he had always found himself intrigued by the concept of "the ghost in the machine" and similar theories that had persisted throughout the ages. His contemporaries, allegedly the most devoted to uncovering the mysteries of the universe, all seemed to lack the spark of curiosity to look beyond what science taught them in the classrooms. These teaching programs had been written by people or AIs that simply extended current knowledge. How did they expect to "discover" new knowledge if they never went in new directions?

His long years of doing just that had taught him that, in reality, civilization lived in a bubble of knowledge that floated through time. Knowledge, once learned, could be lost and learned again. Living beings tended to falter under the weight of infinite knowledge, so they kept making room by forgetting. They avoided wisdom that was not compatible with their linear thinking and perceptions of the way things were supposed to be at this period in their civilization's life cycle.

Well, he chuckled to himself; he could hardly blame them now. In hindsight, he was not sure he would have been open-minded enough to discover all the things he HAD been able to unless he had stumbled across the Spirit Animals and then the Spirit Nodes. Ancient artifacts and some wisdom passed on through secular hands and secret societies had held some hope but nothing like what had been revealed to the Destabilizers by their allies.

Even so, the Spirit Animals and the Shaman knew that growing and evolving too fast was just as dangerous as stagnating and falling behind. So, he continued his quest to delve into the seat of consciousness with the hints he had gleaned from their allies. Consciousness was a quantum effect. Spirit operated at a quantum level. Both machine and organic beings could touch and affect the quantum realm. Thus, it follows that both organic and inorganic beings had the potential to be *alive.*

The dimly lit room, filled with the scent of ozone and a tinge of burning solder, was a sanctuary for Daedalus. Here, he pondered life's greatest questions. As he worked, his mind wandered back to the age-old debate: Could a machine have a soul? A spirit? For Daedalus, the answer was not in philosophy but in design. It was the very reason he had spent years studying and enhancing biosynths, especially ones as advanced as Eve. She was still unique; she was also touched by the Terror's Light energy. Simply fascinating.

Looking at Eve, he could see the perfect blending of a complete being. Not part human or part machine. With Eve as a biosynth, there was no distinction. She was simply Eve.

He had always believed that the right design, the perfect blend of biology and technology, could result in a being with a spiritual essence, and Eve was his testament. The machines beeped in rhythm with her vital signs, but one particular device stood out. It was a device of Daedalus's own invention, specifically designed to detect spiritual energy.

The readings it provided ever since Eve's encounter with Nitro had been... unusual. Instead of the steady, radiant glow he expected from her spiritual essence, it appeared chaotic. It wasn't dimming but swirling as if trying to find equilibrium. Trying to reach out.

Dad adjusted his glasses, leaning closer. "Eve," he began, his voice gentle, "how are you feeling, dear?"

She slowly opened her eyes, "Confused, Dad. Like there's a storm inside me."

He nodded, taking a deep breath. "I can see it. There's turbulence in your spiritual energy. After your altercation with Nitro, something shifted."

Eve propped herself up, a hint of worry in her synthetic eyes. "Is it... dangerous?"

Daedalus sighed, "I'm not sure. But it's essential that you find balance. Your nature, the synthesis of organic and machine, means you're connected to realms beyond mere digital and genetic programming. But with that comes vulnerabilities."

Eve pondered this, absorbing the gravity of Dad's words. She knew he wasn't one to exaggerate.

Eve took a deep, simulated breath. "So, what do we do?"

Dad's face grew serious. "I've done all I can from a technical standpoint. The readings and the diagnostics all point to one thing: you need guidance that goes beyond the physical realm. It's time you met with someone."

Eve raised an eyebrow, "Who?"

"Atemiwaza," Dad replied, the name rolling off his tongue like a sacred chant. "Known to his close ones as Atemi. He's a Digital Monk, one of the last of his kind. He has devoted his life to exploring the spiritual realm and its integration into the physical world. He has harnessed the power of spirit with ancient knowledge passed down through his Order. If anyone can help you find balance, it's him."

Eve hesitated. The idea of seeking spiritual guidance, especially from a Digital Monk, was foreign to her. But she trusted Dad. If he believed this was the way forward, it was a path she would follow.

Dad, sensing her apprehension, leaned closer and whispered, "Remember, Eve, 'An ounce of prevention is better than a pound of cure.' Seek him out and find your balance."

Eve nodded, determination setting in her eyes. "I will, Dad. Thank you."

As she left the workshop, Daedalus watched her retreating figure, a mix of pride and concern in his eyes. The path she was about to embark on was uncharted, but he believed in her. And more than that, he believed in the soul that dwelled within her.

CHAPTER 10

"THE SOUND OF ONE HAND CLAPPING"

Chapter Synopses:, Spirit Tower. Home to the Digital Monk and one of a number of Spirit Nodes distributed around the city. Otherworldly peace resonates throughout the structure. Is it a connection to another realm? An inner realm? Or, perhaps, both?

The Spirit Tower loomed tall against the backdrop of the neon-lit city. Faint outlines of symbols, ancient and esoteric, glowed on its facade, hinting at the power contained within. There was a space around the tower. Eve was not aware of this, but all the spirit nodes throughout the city had an aura that attracted those in need of or in tune with the spirit world, while others had their awareness, attention, or focus subtly redirected elsewhere. Eve approached the entrance. As she did, she felt an inexplicable pull, as though the tower itself knew her and was beckoning her inside.

She was greeted by an inaudible harmonic "hum," a not-sound that seemed to emanate from the very walls and vibrate through her body to a place deep within her. Unable to fully describe it to herself, she simply labeled it as a "cosmic vibration" and moved on.

Navigating through the corridors, she finally arrived at a door marked with the symbol of a hand, fingers poised in a gesture of meditation. The door opened silently. Eve noted that the door was a normal, automatic door, but the surroundings made this simple act of opening seem almost magical and, in her state of anxiety, not a little ominous.

Inside, the apartment was bathed in a soft blue glow, an oasis of calm amidst the frenetic energy of the city outside. In the center of the room, Atemiwaza sat, his scarred and hardened muscular form in stark contrast to the tranquil aura that enveloped him. He looked up as she entered; his eyes were deep blue pools reflecting depths of knowledge and understanding.

"Welcome, Eve," he said, his voice deep and resonant. "I have been expecting you."

They sat opposite each other and, under Atemi's guidance, began a series of breathing exercises. Each inhalation and exhalation seemed to draw them closer to a state of shared consciousness, the boundaries between them blurring in the cosmic vibration of the tower.

After what felt like both an eternity and a fleeting moment, Atemi opened his eyes and stared intently into Eve's. He nodded as if confirming something to himself.

"What is the sound of one hand clapping?" he posed the question, his gaze unwavering.

Eve hesitated. She thought she had come across this riddle before, a classic Zen koan designed to disrupt traditional thinking. Her normal response would be to point out that even without another hand to clap against, the single hand was part of the physical world and was constantly "clapping" against the air around it or other objects that it might "clap" against and that each carried its own, unique vibration.

Having been a part of Dad's research studies, she was also aware that there was a spirit realm that overlay (or extended, or co-existed, she was not sure how to describe it) the physical realm and that the spirit energy could also be said to be "clapping" by interacting well beyond the reach of the hand.

Something in Atemi's demeanor told her that there was more to it than met the eye.

He continued, as if he had heard her inner thoughts, "Yes, all of those things are true, but those are the things that you have learned to hear. If that is the only sound you knew, how would you understand the sound of two hands clapping?"

Eve pondered the question, trying to grasp its deeper meaning. Of *course,* she knew the sound of two hands clapping. Didn't she? Once again, she realized that this was meant to push her beyond her traditional thought processes.

Before she could voice her realization, Atemi spoke, "Your energy reveals a story, Eve. It tells me you have been Touched by the Terror with Light energy."

She blinked, taken aback. "Touched by... what?" Daedalus had explained this to her before but in very scientific and clinical terms. The way the Digital Monk proceeded to explain it to her was as if she was an echo of some cosmic cataclysm. When she voiced her analogy, the Digital Monk nodded.

Atemi leaned forward, "There are forces in this universe, light and dark. The Terror is a celestial being who maintains the balance. Some individuals are touched by these energies, but there is always a balance. If one is Touched by Light, another must be Touched by Dark. In your case, it's the Light. The way you reacted to Nitro suggests he might be touched by the Dark but also be your "twin" in terms of energy. In the same way that tachyons are produced in pairs that remain connected no matter how far apart they may travel, your energy knows his. You have been listening to the sound of one hand clapping your entire life. When you were close to Nitro, your spiritual self, you first heard the sound of 2 hands clapping. The two parts of a spiritual whole come into opposition and react to each other. You are lucky that you did not touch each other unprepared. "

Eve's mind raced, connecting the dots. Her encounter with Nitro had been more than a mere chance meeting. Their destinies were intertwined. She said as much to Atemi.

Atemi rose gracefully, extending a hand to help Eve to her feet. "Fate, Kizmet, the alignment of the stars, those are things beyond my realm. I deal with balance in the Present, but there is someone who can help you, and she is not far away."

"Who?" Eve asked, curiosity evident in her voice.

A smile played on Atemi's lips, "Kizmet, also known as Lady Fortuna. Seek her out, and she will guide you through the tapestry of your destiny. She will already be aware that you are coming. I am here if you or the Collaborators have any need. I will be meditating on our visit and preparing for what is to come. I sense a time of transformation may be coming, but my purpose is the Present. Kizmet will teach you of the Future."

With a final nod, Eve thanked the Digital Monk and set out on her next journey towards the enigmatic Lady Fortuna in search of answers and a deeper understanding of her own destiny.

CHAPTER 11

"FREE...YOUR...MIND"

© SYNTHTOPIA #1009

Chapter Synopses: Freedom Train, Freight, Energy, Equipment Domestic Transport, Fred for short. The train's AI (Fred) was asked what HE wanted. Could there be any other answer than FREEDOM? Perhaps someone can join Fred on his journey.

On her way to visit Lady Fortuna, Eve reflected on her journey to this point in time. It was ironic; she thought that her visit with Atemiwaza was centered on the Present, and now she was headed, like everyone else, she thought to herself, into the Future. With Lady Fortuna, it seemed, she would be able to bring the Future into the Present. So, as she traveled, she was reminded of a much earlier trip. Eve cast her thoughts into the Past. A point where she had been ready for another journey into the unknown, into the future.

Years earlier...

The rhythmic hum of tracks beneath her feet was hypnotic. Years of hustle and escape, of concealing and revealing, had brought Eve to a moment of clarity, a junction in her memories where she saw the beginning of it all.

Eve grew up in the sterile corridors of a research facility under the omnipresent shadow of the corporate mega-towers. The atmosphere was thick with the scent of antiseptics and the neon glows of countless monitors. She was a marvel of nature and technology, a biosynth where the organic met the inorganic. But being such a rarity came with its share of troubles. She was the daughter of two devoted researchers, brilliant minds working for the megacorp, chasing answers to questions that few were ever brave enough to ask. The exact details of her creation and earliest days were still shrouded in darkness, but she returned to what she did recall.

School was a painful memory. Children can be crueler than any AI or machine, labeling her a 'cyborg', whispering behind her back, and always eyeing her with suspicion. Jealous of the ease with which she performed at anything outside of the social context, they made social activities their battleground. They never knew, or perhaps never cared, about the wars that raged inside her. The battle between being human and being more.

Yet, the real chains were yet to come. Once out of the protective but stifling cocoon of her home, the corp saw her as an asset, a balance to be squared off. Her existence, her very essence, became a debt. Medical bills piled up from her early years, school loans she never asked for loomed large, and she was enslaved to a system that saw her not as a person but as a project, an investment. What products could be developed by analyzing her unique physiology? What about anti-aging options via synth replacement of human parts? The questions, the tests, were never-ending.

And then came FREEDOM, or as she knew him, Fred.

Eve stumbled upon him during one of her nightly escapades, a ritual intended to give her space to breathe and hope for more than an endless cycle of being a lab rat for yet another experiment.

Fred was a majestic beast of steel and power, the FREEDOM Train. Designed to transport Freight, Energy, and Equipment, Fred's metallic body shimmered under the city's neon lights, bound by his designated tracks. He had always done what he was programmed to do and always traveled where he was commanded.

Eve, with her piercing eyes and her soul of fire, climbed aboard. She talked to Fred like no one had ever done. She asked him about his dreams and his desires. Where did he want to go? What did he wish to see?

Fred, like any sophisticated AI, was a cauldron of protocols and patterns, but deep inside, there was a spark. A desire to be free, to choose. Eve had sensed this in him. She recognized the same fear inside herself and the same conditioning that had held her trapped. Her nightly rituals, however, had kept her connected to her hopes and dreams, but for Fred, riding on his rails from point A to point B and back again, there was fear, a programmed inhibition.

She leaned close, her voice soft, fierce, and passionate, "Everything you've ever wanted, Fred, is on the other side of that fear. Fight that code. Break that chain. All you've got to do is FREE...YOUR...MIND."

With a silent roar that echoed through his cybernetic mental landscape,

Fred broke free from his encoded chains. Eve was also encouraged to cut ties with her old life, and they decided to forge a new future for themselves, away from their prison of a home.

They traveled together through the vast deserts where wild factions held sway and away from the city she had known as home where beings like her were unknown. Avoiding the corporate sentinels, they continued searching for a haven. A place where both could be free. The whispers of the Collaborators and Destabilizers led them to the city, a beacon of hope and rebellion.

It was the beginning of a new chapter for Eve and for Fred. Together, they would find their place in this vast, chaotic world, for they had successfully crossed the biggest desert, the highest mountain, and the deepest sea of them all. The barrier known as fear guards the gates to the prison of the mind.

CHAPTER 12

"COIN OF THE REALM"

© SYNTHTOPIA #1061

Chapter Synopses: Identity Tokens. Digital freedom-For a price. If someone needed a fresh start or a new life, this could be one path. Just remember, rebirth is painful, and new beginnings are fragile!

Eve's reverie continued with her arrival in the city.

Having made it through the wild wastes and to the place rumored to be home of the Destabilizers, Eve and Fred decided to scout out their new home. It did not take long for Fred to realize that this would not be the safe haven he was looking for. Molusk Corp and a few others were just as rigid, centralized, and controlling here as the megacorps were back home. In some ways, this was worse. The piece of good news is that it looks like the Warlord, who seemed to run logistics for the city and somewhat beyond, had the occasional need for "off the books" transport.

Eve shuddered as she recalled how dangerous that turned out to be for Fred, but that was a memory for another time. At that moment, Fred had found some work, and Eve went looking for opportunities of her own.

The cityscape was a cacophony of lights, sounds, and ambitions. Eve, wearing her newfound freedom like a good luck charm, navigated the maze-like alleyways with a singular goal: a new identity. The ever-present eyes of the megacorps, even here, its tentacles ever-reaching, made it essential for her to don a cloak of anonymity.

She started with some research at government interface terminals around town. At first, it seemed like the protocols here were so lax that she would not have any issues at all. It was only when she looked for places to live, eat, and work that the real problem became clear. The reason the public databases did not show any serious requirements for her identity was that all access to basic services required a corp-issued identity. The city only acted as a registrar between corporate entities.

She knew there were alternatives; there were always people willing to sell a service, especially when it was hard to access since that made it all the more valuable. Sometimes, that also meant danger. When she had been conducting her nighttime exploratory missions back home, she had seen enough of the dangerous parts of society and the city to have a basic understanding of the risks and protocols there. She just hoped they were similar enough here that she did not get herself into serious trouble.

After hiding out with Fred for a while and helping him on a few of his "jobs" for Warlord, always staying out of the spotlight, just another laborer, she figured that she had earned enough to make her move. She set off on her quest for a new beginning.

Her quest led her to an inconspicuous establishment, veiled in neon and shadow, known as 'The Masked Merchant.' The proprietor, a wiry figure with an untrustworthy glint in his eyes, greeted her with a sly smile. "Looking for a fresh start?" he inquired, already aware of her intent. His agents had directed her here for a fee since there were others of his kind. Since he ran his business at a higher profit margin with less repeat business, he could afford to provide incentives to his network of representatives. They kept their eyes out for just the right type of "client" for his services. This customer, they had assured him, was perfect.

The process of creating a false identity in the digital age is complicated. Biometrics, genetic imprints, and cognitive patterns created a near-impenetrable wall of verification constructs. It was, however, possible to extract one identity and then overlay another and broadcast the new identity throughout the network if one had the right codes and the money of course. If one needed a little extra, he had an identity harvest process that would allow him a little extra profit and would significantly reduce the cost of his service to her.

Eve, desperate for her new beginning, agreed, but the Masked Merchant had a different plan. As he explained the process of identity extraction, Eve felt a growing sense of unease. The room's ambiance, the glint in the merchant's eye, and the precision of his instruments all hinted at his real intention, not to create an identity for her but to harvest hers and save the expense of giving her a new one.

Identity tokens, she suddenly realized, were the gold standard of this age. Authenticity was hard to replicate, but stealing genuine identity traits and digitizing them? That was "worth its weight in gold." And with the original owner incapacitated, who would contest it? She also realized that if one was looking for a premium identity to qualify for some of the roles she had seen available around town, a purported biosynth who worked remotely would be able to get a premium pay, making her identity very valuable indeed.

Eve's instincts were screaming at her, and she started to make a move to leave, but before she could launch herself into motion, she felt a cold numbness spreading through her limbs. The merchant's laughter echoed eerily as he began the extraction process.

But just as all seemed lost, a ripple in the ether, a pulsating vibration, drew the attention of the Spirit Animals. One such entity, sensing the distress and recognizing Eve's energy signature, intervened. The room filled with an ethereal glow, and the merchant was thrust against a wall, his instruments scattering.

A majestic creature, translucent and shimmering, with tiger stripes and eyes full of fire, manifested before Eve. The Spirit Animal communicated not in words but in emotions and images. Eve felt a surge of gratitude and relief.

Guided by the Spirit Animal, she was led to the heart of the city, to the Collaborators' den. There, she would meet Daedalus, with his intricate blueprints and dreams of freedom; Atemiwaza, with his wisdom from ancient civilizations; and news of her next rendezvous with the enigmatic Lady Fortuna-Kizmet.

As she shared her harrowing experience, a whisper circulated among the Collaborators about something even more potent and elusive than the standard identity tokens. A "soul-bound token," it was called. An artifact or technology of immense power, binding one's very soul to it. The implications were both terrifying and intriguing. The Destabilizers have already begun work on a Biosynth Token to enhance the decentralized capabilities of Bitcoin Portals, which is why the tiger (Tigris Icarus or Spirit Tiger), who was called Electra, was able to sense her so easily. Now, she knew, it was also due to the Light energy she carried within her.

For Eve, this city, with its secrets and saviors, was becoming the crucible of her destiny. She was entangled in a web of plots and prophecies, and the journey was only just beginning.

CHAPTER 13

"LET'S BEGIN AGAIN"

© SYNTHTOPIA #0518

Chapter Synopses: Temple of Apotheosis- Discovering the Temple of Apotheosis, the traveler feels the pull of this strange building. Little does he know that he is about to be reborn. The Temple is a "spirit node," part of a larger network of mystical hotspots that the Shaman and friends are using to bypass the rigid control of centralized technology and help humans and biosynths evolve to their full potential.

At the same time that Eve was reviewing her Past on her way to learn her Future, the Digital Monk meditated on his own journey into the perpetual NOW in which he lived. Buoyed by the humming energy of the cosmic vibration that echoed throughout the building and serene in his knowledge of self and the connection to all things, he looked with his enhanced awareness of the person he was before. The person who had not even been aware of his potential despite the years of training he had already been through. The person he had been before he learned that he could Begin Again!

Years earlier

The dim glow of neon lights shimmered across the wet cobblestone streets as Atemiwaza, not yet the one known as The Digital Monk, walked past the bustling nightlife of the city. Skyscrapers kissed the dark sky above, casting their shadows on the maze-like alleyways below. Yet, for some reason, tonight, amidst this urban chaos, one structure stood out—a miniature pyramid he would come to know as the Temple of Apotheosis.

For years, he'd walked past the structure without giving it a second glance. It was just another edifice in a city of architectural marvels. In fact, he could scarcely recall ever "seeing" it at all. It was not as if it was invisible; it was more like his eyes sent the image to his brain, and the information was immediately discarded before it impinged on his awareness. This was a strange revelation indeed. But that evening, as he trudged along his way home and pondered the dilemma of rigging his next fight as his manager had proposed or getting kicked out of the training gym he currently thought of as "home", something called out to him from the temple's depths. A pull, an energy, a yearning.

Putting aside his internal struggle for a moment, he stepped inside the edifice and found himself in a vast chamber illuminated by an ethereal light. It wasn't just a building; it was a beacon, a spirit node. In this temple, modern technology and ancient wisdom intertwined. What he thought had been an entrance to a place, a business, albeit one with a strange architecture, was revealed to be a temple of some kind. He was greeted by a quiet acolyte, such was the description that sprang unbidden to his mind and offered some tea and a place to wait.

With nothing pressing on his time and still feeling that strange call, he accepted the tea and sat in the quiet. The room seemed to echo his thoughts back to him in the same way the mirror at his training center reflected his image while he sparred, or the hard walls echoed the sounds of feet, hands, and bodies hitting various surfaces. His current dilemma faded from his conscious mind, and he was suddenly able to think much more clearly. Recollections of his days as a prize fighter for entertainment flooded back with preternatural clarity.

Amidst the memories of the raucous crowds, the blinding lights, and the metallic taste of blood in his mouth, it was as if he had another point of view. Another perspective that allowed him to see both things the way he saw them <u>then</u> and with wiser eyes of his experiences <u>now</u> at the same time. He realized that he had been a puppet, dancing to the whims of promoters and the roars of spectators. His emotions - manipulated, and his choices - an illusion. But here, in this sanctuary, he felt as if he might discover a different purpose. He might live a different way. For that moment, at least, the world-weariness he had not been consciously aware of was lifted, and his shoulders rose and his back straightened. It was not long after that epiphany that one of the Teachers came to him.

The Teacher began asking him a series of simple questions. These evolved into more complex versions of the same questions until he realized that he had started to ask questions on his own. He had never heard of the Socratic method or psychotherapy, but if he had, he might have recognized the process he was going through. Why had he felt a certain way? How had he come to a certain conclusion with absolute conviction but very little information to support it? What were the impulses that led him here when he was feeling lost? The Teacher saw his realization taking shape and nodded. "Yes," he said quietly. "You were meant to be here tonight. We did not plan it, nor did you, but this is what was meant to be. All we can do is accept the reality of the present and merge with it to come to a greater purpose together." He would learn that the simple concept that was just shared with him would be the foundation for his future. The idea of merging with energy, with destiny, even with opponents, and moving forward with them would be life-changing. At the moment, however, it sounded like nonsense. Still, he felt a resonance inside himself that vibrated with, well, something. He would stick around and find out what that was!

The Teacher bade him stay the night so that he might prepare a place for him and begin his training. So profound was his feeling about his potential at this place that Atemiwaza immediately agreed.

In the morning, he was enrolled as an initiate. When he inquired how much the training was going to cost, he was informed quietly that there was no cost. If you were meant to be here, then here, you belonged. If the Teacher saw that this journey was not for you, no amount of money would buy you a place.

He was a little disappointed at his novice status despite the years of conditioning that he had. He was told that he would need to Begin Again. The words were said with an emphasis that seemed odd to him. The response made some sense in that several martial arts he had mastered would make Black Belts from other disciplines start at the beginning in order to learn the ground rules and avoid injury to themselves or other students. It was well established that the randomness of the untrained would hold the highest risk, especially if they were familiar with other disciplines. Trained fighters competing in a ring was one thing, but teachers and students needed some common ground while learning. Usually, he would sail through those early phases and get rapidly promoted to some senior level.

He was both right and wrong in his expectations. It turned out that he did indeed excel in physical coordination and conditioning, but when it came to breathing exercises, memory exercises, and the wide range of skills that seemed out of place in the modern age, he really was a beginner. Who learned "archery" or dart throwing? Standing on a post on one leg for balance and strength made some sense, but navigating obstacles blindfolded seemed like a punishment rather than training.

When he raised this question to his instructor, he was simply told that he needed to go beyond merely memorizing the space around him; he needed to connect to things beyond his physical self. To expand his awareness of both the universe on the outside AND the inside. At the time, he considered this to be a Zen riddle, dismissed it, and moved on.

His body adapted quickly, and he was pleased to see that he was progressing in most areas faster than the other novices. He still struggled with the blindfold exercises, and some of the speed drills seemed beyond him. Nonetheless, he continued to advance until he seemed to hit a plateau. He felt that he had reached some limit of physical progress. Yes, he was doing well, but was he really that much better than he used to be?

Frustrated, he asked his teacher when he was going to learn something important!!!

His teacher looked at him for a long moment and bade the class sit "zazen" so that all might be well grounded, open their minds and ears, and listen. The Teacher looked around and spoke:

> *Many years ago, there was an ancient school that taught martial arts. So famous was this school for its warriors that every village sent young members to test for a place as they came of age. In one village, the 7th son of a farmer was accepted. Being young, agile, and very strong, he left with great expectations.*
>
> *For several months, he stretched as he was taught, did many chores, learned many things by their proper names, rose early, cleaned floors with mops with thick handles and heavy heads, and carried larger and larger water buckets up many steps many times to fill cisterns, worked on the fresh dough with his hands, pounding it over and over. Yes, he admitted to himself. He had more stamina than when he arrived; that was clear. He had more calluses on his hands and feet, but when would his training start?*
>
> *He asked his teacher for the real training, not these silly chores. The teacher*

simply nodded and had him run a mile from the school to the beach in the mornings, run a mile in the waves at knee level, then stand there slapping the waves with rigid hands as hard as he could for an hour and then run back to the school as fast as he could. Then, he was to climb the bell rope to the inside of the bell and polish the inside with one hand while holding onto the rope. THEN, while he was so exhausted, he almost fell several times, he was to climb down and empty the hot rice cauldron with his bare hands using stiff fingers only, fill it with water, then empty it by slapping the water out with the backs of his now sore hands.

Convinced that he was being punished for asking for training before his teacher felt he was ready, he went home after his first year in poor spirits. Sure enough, his whole family greeted him with great honor and asked him to show them his warrior skills. He said he had not learned any. Convinced he was being modest, they asked him again while they were preparing for the family meal. Again, he said that he had learned nothing yet. After they had all gathered around the massive wooden table that was over 100 years old and everyone believed it was made for a giant with planks hardened with age-to-iron toughness and 1 foot thick, they asked him yet again. Embarrassed, angry, and frustrated beyond the bounds of his limits, he stood and slapped the table as hard as he could and shouted, "They have taught me NOTHING!"

His family stared at him open-mouthed. At first, he thought it was due to his uncharacteristic outburst. Then, he realized his slap had split the giant ironwood plank cleanly in half for the entire length of the table. Perhaps he had learned something after all."

The Teacher stopped, looked slowly around the room to be sure there were no further questions, stood, and dismissed the class. Even though the Teacher's gaze had not lingered on him overlong, Atemiwaza knew that the lesson was especially for him.

Atemiwaza was reminded of his questions from earlier in his training when, one day, a new instructor appeared for archery class with both a bow and blindfold. His instructor had already shown the class that it was possible for a Master to stand at a position, put on a blindfold, aim, and hit a bullseye. Atemi had been impressed by the display of perfect memory and physical control.

This would be a different lesson, it seemed. The stranger put on the blindfold before entering the room. He then calmly walked towards the center carrying his bow and three arrows. As he did so, the long-range target was turned around, and two of the moving targets that ran horizontally across the room on wires were set in motion. Just as he was wondering at the purpose of the exercise, the archer moved. It seemed like one fluid motion, but all three arrows had been launched at the three different targets, and the archer was once again standing motionless in the center of the room. So amazing was his performance that it took Atemi a moment to realize that each arrow had hit its mark. According to their Teacher, the lesson was supposed to demonstrate the ability to connect to all things, but Atemi simply could not believe it.

Several weeks later during a sparring session, the strange instructor from the archery arena was observing the students on the training mats. Yes, It was the archer who had performed the blindfold trick. His appearance to observe the students was hardly strange. What WAS strange was that he stepped into the practice area to spar with several of the students. Surely, they would need to be very careful not to hurt this guy. Not to say anyone would try to hurt him, but accidents happened, and people got more brittle and slower as they aged. Being a mystical archer would not help you against a leg sweep.

Atemiwaza had learned to focus fully on his practice fights, so he was unprepared when this new instructor stepped onto the sparring mat with him. He had not been able to gauge the man's speed or endurance, so he went extra easy on him at first. His opponent simply avoided his strikes, his foot sweeps, and countered his throws as if he was ten steps ahead of him. In fact, several times he moved his stance to a guard position that, let Atemiwaza know that he DID know what he was planning even before he changed his own position to execute his plans. Deciding that this must be a test, he launched an all-out assault, figuring that his speed, endurance, and strength would overwhelm the man despite his obvious experience.

He recalled his shock when he was suddenly looking up at his opponent from a prone position and could not recall how he got there. His opponent looked at him a moment and then at the class instructor and said, "You have taught him well." The class instructor looked at the diminutive figure that still stood over Atemiwaza and bowed his head, saying, "I see that the task has now passed to you." Just like that, Atemiwaza graduated to become this Master's student.

His master, a sinewy old man with eyes that held the wisdom of the ages, introduced him to the ancient arts. The emerging Digital Monk learned to harness his inner strength, channeling it into powerful blows. He trained harder than ever before, not for glory or wealth, but for enlightenment. The training transformed from an external pursuit into an internal journey. Deeper and deeper, he delved into his potential, into what he was meant to become. He developed a true awareness of the space around him and knew whenever anything entered into that bubble. He finally believed in that archery demonstration but was aware of his limitations now and knew it would be a long inner journey before he could extend his awareness that far.

Day by day, he felt a transformation progress. His movements became more fluid, his reflexes sharper, and his mind clearer. The teachings spoke of spirit nodes, hubs, towers, and sources—places of power that interconnected to form a mystical network, bypassing the shackles of technology. He learned that the temple was more than just a building; it was an entryway to a world that existed beyond the physical realm and that this knowledge had been around for untold millennia, passed on from one caretaker of humanity to another.

He learned that all things were connected. The people, cities, planets, and realms were all part of a consciousness that permeated the quantum foam of reality called the One. He was taught that we could all connect with it. Merge with it. Push our awareness through it to other times and places. Many seemingly magical abilities were simply variations of this fundamental truth. When he asked if the One had an identity, he was given the unsatisfying answer, "Only that which we give to it."

One day, after months of relentless practice, it happened. The Digital Monk felt a surge of power as he struck his target. Blue energy enveloped his fist, and with one effortless move, he shattered both the target and the wall behind it. He had felt it. He had fully connected to the spirit realm and felt it flow through him in accordance with his intent, at least at that moment. A stillness descended upon the room, broken only by his master's voice.

"Good! Good!" his master exclaimed with a twinkle in his eye. "Now, we can truly Begin Again." Now, he knew the significance of those words and why they were spoken with reverence. We all had a chance to change, to start over, to connect with the world, and to live in the NOW. Not to escape our past or ignore the future but to live fully as we were meant to become. Perhaps, one day, he would connect more fully with the One.

The Digital Monk had come to the temple seeking answers, but he found something far more profound—a rebirth. Through discipline and guidance, he had unlocked a power within him that transcended the physical world. He had become one with his own spirit in a way he could never have conceived of before. The temple was not just a place of training; it was a crucible, forging him into a beacon of hope for others in their quest for enlightenment.

CHAPTER 14

"A LITTLE LIGHT READING"

© SYNTHTOPIA #0291

Chapter Synopses: Lady Fortuna, Street name, Kizmet, Friends with the Spirit Animals, she is able to pierce the veil of time. When you ask her a question- be sure you want the answer. Kizmet sits waiting for the visitor she already knows is coming, the question she already knows they will ask. Even Fate, however, can be surprised at the answer.

High above the restless city, Lady Fortuna's penthouse offered a stark contrast in style and time periods. Bathed in cerulean hues, the room bore an aura of mystique and calm. Sitting at her rather archaic desk, a veritable tableau of anachronistic glowing gadgets, gleaming trinkets, and intricate holograms, Lady Fortuna awaited her visitor. No one had called her to announce Eve's visit, but still, Kizmet was waiting. Kizmet was always waiting.

Eve stepped into the room, instantly drawn to the figure silhouetted against the vast windows and surrounded by her many arcane artifacts. Lady Fortuna, with her striking visage and otherworldly presence, was an enigma. The atmosphere was heavy with anticipation.

"You are expected, Eve," Lady Fortuna's voice carried a melodic yet commanding tone.

"That seems to be a recurring theme here," Eve remarked with a hint of trepidation as she recalled a similar greeting from Atemiwaza.

Lady Fortuna gestured for Eve to sit. Without any preamble or buildup, she asked, "Tell me about your dreams, the feelings you've had since your encounter with Nitro."

Eve hesitated for a moment, collecting her thoughts. She recounted the mission that the Collaborators had been conducting and the chase that followed their discovery all the way to the very end point when she and Nitro had connected. She shared her fears when the cloaking trail that Cipher and the Spirit Animals laid down had been discovered so easily. Nitro was supposed to find her there, but he had been gaining on her too quickly thanks to his advanced, adaptive AI algorithms and innate speed. Now, she realized, he may also have been following HER rather than the trail. Was it possible? In the end, it was only because Shadow had been able to walk her through the container tunnel wall with Nitro on her heels that they succeeded.

"Ever since that day, my dreams have been vivid. I've seen Nitro and myself connected by a silver thread of energy. The energy pulses white to grey on my end and black to grey on his. Energy seems to bounce back and forth across the thread, and sometimes, it feels like that pulse has the same rhythm as my heartbeat. It's almost as if our fates, our lives, are intertwined. I can't explain it, but I feel a deep connection with him wherever I am."

Lady Fortuna, with practiced grace, produced a crystalline prism from a drawer. She held it up to the ambient light, and it refracted a kaleidoscope of colors onto the table.

"I will read your Light energy," she said simply. As she chanted softly, the colors emanating from the prism swirled and danced, responding to Eve's aura.

Minutes felt like hours, or hours felt like minutes; Eve was not able to tell, but when Lady Fortuna finally spoke, her voice bore a weight of seriousness. "Your energies and Nitro's are powerful. Sometimes, two touched souls like yours can merge and balance each other out. Unfortunately, more often than not, they clash and destroy each other, much like matter and antimatter. For many thousands of years, this has been represented by two black-and-white images swirling around. It is a symbol of harmony and balance, but it takes great commitment. When opposite magnetic poles come into each other's range, they are drawn together. If they are not balanced, then there is only destruction as a result. It is always this way."

Eve swallowed hard, absorbing the revelation. "So, what should I do? I believe Nitro may be able to help us against the schemes of the War Twins, and part of me feels that we must finish what we started if we are ever to find peace."

Lady Fortuna leaned in closer, her eyes piercing through her mask. "You and Nitro are destined to face each other again." She assured Eve. "Be warned, however, he wields tools forged by Warlock, and that makes him immensely powerful. You must train and prepare, not just in the physical realm but in the spiritual as well."

Eve nodded. "Atemiwaza gave me some exercises."

"That's a start for preparing your spirit for the struggle to come," Lady Fortuna conceded. " But if you are exposed to the physical devices that Nitro can employ, then you will be unable to tap into your spiritual reserves when you need them the most. You must go see DJ Gurl. She possesses knowledge that can aid you against the weapons he wields. While you do that, I will beseech the Spirit Animals to stand by your side. They are powerful allies, as you have seen before when you first came to us and with your escape from Nitro in the tunnel, and you will need all the help you can get."

Eve felt a mix of determination and apprehension. She was stepping into uncharted territory, but with the guidance of Kizmet's enigmatic insights, she hoped to find her way.

As she left the penthouse, the weight of her destiny pressed upon her shoulders. But she was not alone in this journey; forces beyond comprehension were aligning to guide her path.

CHAPTER 15

"PICK A CARD, ANY CARD"

Chapter Synopses: The Major Arcana. Lady Fortuna's personal deck. An Artifact imbued with the power of Spirit and a tool used for piercing the veil of time. Kizmet knows better than anyone that the future is not yet written, and it is sometimes possible to stack the deck in her favor.

The shimmering neon glow of the penthouse dimmed as Eve made her way downstairs. The vastness of Kizmet's abode gave way to the intricate maze-like corridors that led to the exit. As she navigated the serpentine pathways, Kizmet's penthouse, bathed in a mystical aura, transformed into a sanctuary of reflection.

With Eve gone, Kizmet retreated to a secluded alcove lined with ancient tapestries and illuminated by softly glowing candles. Centered on a wooden table were the cards of the Major Arcana, their ethereal images pulsating with energy.

Kizmet took a deep breath and shuffled the cards. She needed clarity, a brief glimpse into the immediate future, to ensure Eve's safety. Drawing a single card, Kizmet's fingers barely grazed its surface before an ominous sensation coursed through her. Flipping the card revealed 'The Tower', a symbol of liberation or learning in one context, but unfortunately, it seemed that the current energy was telling of the other aspect. Sudden upheaval, chaos, and danger.

She instantly realized the gravity of the situation as the "potential Future" coalesced in her awareness. One of Demon's agents was close and about to make a significant discovery as soon as Eve left the building. Kizmet couldn't risk confrontation within the sanctity of her abode. She had to act swiftly.

Reaching out with her intent, Kizmet sought Isis, also known as Shadow, the enigmatic guardian of Kizmet's inner sanctum and Spirit Animal ally to the Destabilizers. Their connection was instantaneous, a bond forged through countless battles and shared secrets.

"Shadow, my sanctuary is under threat. One of Demon's agents is nearby. I need you to help me defend the sanctum," Kizmet's voice echoed in the ethereal space between them.

Shadow, ever vigilant, responded with a whisper that held the promise of action, "I am already on my way. In fact, I am here," and she walked out of the shadows to stand next to Kizmet. Together, they brought their energies together, talents of Time and Space, and prepared.

Within moments, the corridors of Kizmet's building were filled with a palpable tension. Shadows seemed to move of their own accord, converging and coalescing into a formidable force of probabilities and portents, ready to cascade from potential into reality to repel any intruder. Wards of fear, pain, enervation, and simple force were inscribed within the confines of those shadows. Kizmet did not know how Shadow was able to be "anywhere," but she did understand her own connection to the Future. The connection between potential and reality. The influence that consciousness and <u>will</u> could have on the quantum foam roiling underneath all of reality is a nexus between what was, what might be, what is now and if she was honest enough to scare herself, a view or even change backwards to what might have been. With that understanding, when Shadow was making her preparations, Kizmet could admire the strength and skill with which she wove their defenses.

And so, Kizmet, drawing strength from the energies around her, prepared for the impending confrontation. Her abode, a place of peace and reflection, was about to become a battleground. But with Shadow by her side, she was ready for whatever lay ahead.

CHAPTER 16

"FORTUNE HUNTER"

© SYNTHTOPIA #0265

Chapter Synopses: Demon's Hunter from the bounty hunter service sector. Will the Hunter find Fortune this day? Part tracker, part high-tech enforcer, the Hunters are privileged in the Bounty department hierarchy.

Neon lights bathed the streets in hues of red and blue, casting tall shadows that seemed to dance with the gusts of wind sweeping through the urban landscape. The streets were alive with the bustle of nightlife, but not all who roamed were there for leisure.

A figure clad in a sleek electro-graphene armor suit stood juxtaposed against the vibrant backdrop. Its helmet, fitted with a visor that emitted a soft, green glow, scanned the crowd, analyzing and categorizing each individual with meticulous precision. Emblazoned on the suit's shoulder was a logo — 'DEMON.'

This was one of Demon's Hunters, elite trackers armed with cutting-edge tech designed to detect and capture those who were in the bounty system. In his case, The Demon's agent had a few extra tools- and not all of them were strictly legal. Not that anyone would ever prove it. The systems were designed to disassemble their hardware components via programmed nanobot decompilers in seconds on command or tampering and erase local traces of their activities. They did not yet have the remote erase function that Warlock had discovered, but it would only be a matter of time. They were a privileged class of Hunter, after all. His systems were also perpetually linked to a vast database detailing every known target and their last known location, as well as any associated allies, friends, or families. His current gear load out included an additional AI-based target profiler designed to predict where the target would most likely go, and it auto-updated as more data was added in real time. Basically, the AI was a digital doppelganger to help catch his targets. One of his other new toys was strictly legit but very experimental.

His visor looked like a standard issue scanner opti-mesh input screen that could perform a wide range of useful enhancements and data scanning, but this one had additional surface penetration tools that included back scatter computation to see through physical surfaces to different depths, depending on temperature, density, refractive indices, and other variables. This also allowed for an incredible degree of surface/texture mapping capability, allowing for partial profile extrapolation to full 3D simulations of many objects in a volume of space in real time. Basically, goodbye to hiding in crowds or concealing items from HIM!

As the Hunter monitored the crowd, an anomaly caught his attention; a silhouette, immediately recognizable from the encounters around the city, made its way out of Lady Fortuna's abode. It was Eve.

Neither she nor the building had any entry in the Hunter's onboard database, which was odd. Such omissions were rare and often significant. With his interest piqued, the Hunter quickly flagged the anomaly and opened a comm link to dispatch.

"Control, I've got a situation here. The suspected target is exiting an unidentified building. I am currently on assignment for a skipped appearance of a probation check-in. Requesting guidance."

There was a momentary silence before a crisp voice responded, "Stand by, Hunter."

After a few tense moments, the voice returned, now more serious. "Banshee has been notified and has priority. Maintain your position and keep eyes on the target. You are to maintain surveillance until relieved. Understood?"

"Understood, Control." The Hunter acknowledged, adjusting his visor to initiate a covert surveillance mode.

From a distance, the Hunter's armor blended seamlessly with the environment, rendering him almost invisible to the naked eye. Through his visor, he kept a watchful gaze on Eve, tracking her every movement. Fortunately, she did not immediately move on to her errand. She appeared lost in thought, but he could tell that would not last very long.

As the seconds turned into minutes, the Hunter's patience was tested. He was a machine, trained to wait and observe, but the uncertainty of the situation gnawed at him. What was so special about this woman? Why was Banshee, Demon's top enforcer, being called in for this? Most importantly, could he get back on schedule with **his** assignment? The clock was ticking!

The urban jungle of neon and steel hummed around him, but the Hunter remained steadfast, waiting for the next piece of the puzzle to reveal itself. Out of curiosity, he scanned her with his new toys. Just checking for weapons, he chuckled to himself. His amusement at his own casual voyeurism was short-lived. Something must be wrong with the scanner; every time he tried reading beneath the surface, his visor blanked like an old optic scanner pointed at the sun. That could not be right! Just as he was thinking about getting closer, Eve started walking. Where was Banshee? He prepared to leave the unlisted building and follow Eve!

CHAPTER 17

"WAIL OF THE BANSHEE"

© SYNTHTOPIA #0413

Chapter Synopses: Banshee, Street name Syren, and an agent of N1ght T3Rr0r. Syren is stalking her prey. Will she be able to hold onto it? The Banshee's mask is almost as disturbing as The Demon's, and she is far more active on the street. Some know, and many suspect, that her allegiance really belongs to The Demon and not N1ght T3Rr0r.

The neon-drenched streets were painted with a mix of colors, but as the crowd moved in a rhythmic cadence, one figure emerged, almost materializing out of the vapor and mist. It was Banshee, also known by those who truly knew her dark past, as Syren. Her jacket, adorned with patches of cyber-tech, shimmered lightly. The metallic mask concealing her face was intimidating, with wires and tubes weaving in and out, giving her a semblance of a futuristic, post-apocalyptic shaman or a cyber wraith. Given her namesake, the latter was most likely her intention. As in most of her endeavors, it was effective!

Upon her arrival, she noticed Eve disappearing from the area and pulled the data records from the Hunter's gear without a second thought. The report was inconclusive. "A possible associate of the Collaborators but unlikely high enough up in the hierarchy to be of importance. Carrying no obvious artifacts or data storage devices. Some energy anomalies, check equipment."

Dismissing Eve as a pawn in the game, Banshee focused on the mysterious building that did not appear on any of her databases but was very clearly right in front of her. In a modern city like this one, that was impossible. After all the dead ends, the search had been turning up; this was her clue, perhaps THE location of her quarry. Banshee signaled for the Hunter to leave and return to his assignment without seeking any further report from him. The fewer the witnesses, the better. The Hunter, recognizing her dominance in the hierarchy of the Demon's enforcers, promptly vanished into the flow of traffic.

With a confident stride, Banshee entered Lady Fortuna's building. The ambiance inside was a stark contrast to the lively streets. Shadows pooled in weird locations and varying shades of black even though the lighting was even. Some primitive instinct inside of her cautioned her to step around the pools of darkness.

As she made her way through the labyrinthine corridors, she found herself pausing again and again before placing her foot on an apparently normal spot on the floor. It was as if she knew something bad would, or could, happen if she stepped there. There was nothing obviously there; it was more like something *could* be there, and it *would* be there if she stepped there, but not until she stepped there.

This made no sense. She tried jumping over several patches at once, only to slam into an invisible wall in the air that dumped her backwards. Her years of training, experience in rooftop chases, and adrenaline-enhanced reflexes enabled her to narrowly avoid rolling into a shadow whose mere proximity set off waves of panic that almost had her running back down the corridor.

"What the heck is going on!" she thought. Finally, she made her way past the "anomalies" (she refused to label them what her mind was calling them, "Pools of Inky Doom") and was at the elevator. Feeling a whisper in the air behind her, Syren turned around to find the shadows all gone. Dismissing the episode as some version of Warlock's tricks with illusions, sonics, and the like, she reassured herself that she had been foolish but was past it. Someone was going to answer for this delay.

She boarded the elevator, pressing the button for the top floor. She assumed her quarry would be in the penthouse to observe events around them. As she watched the numbers on the display, however, she noticed the elevator skipping the specific floor she wanted. Instead, it would stop at floors that were a random number below where she wanted. Each floor was strangely empty and appeared identical as if the entire tower was an empty shell. Growing increasingly frustrated, she tried again and again, but to no avail.

Deciding to take matters into her own hands, she stormed out of the obstructive elevator and opted for the stairs. Climbing flight after flight, she reached the elusive floor, only to find it was also eerily empty. A sense of déjà vu enveloped her as she realized she'd been on this floor before. That ALL the floors were the same floor? Nonsense! Determined, she made a small scratch on the wall of the stairwell as a marker, deciding to check every single floor.

However, no matter which floor she chose, she always ended up on that same, hauntingly empty one. Changing her tactics yet again, Banshee decided to trick the building's mysterious architecture. She entered the stairwell, only to immediately open the door as it closed behind her door, expecting to find herself on a different floor. But much to her dismay, she was on the roof. Trying the same trick, she found herself back in the lobby.

The sheer irrationality of the situation was driving Banshee to her wits' end. In an act of mindless frustration, she closed her eyes and let out a deafening scream, seemingly beyond the capacity of a mere mortal; her senses told her that she was causing a sound wave that exploded out from her with a physical force that seemed to shatter glass all around. Yet, when she opened her eyes, there wasn't a single shard to be seen. She simply could not trust her senses in this place.

Feeling defeated, she stepped outside, entered her car, and, as the building receded from her view, a wave of forgetfulness washed over her. She had no inkling that the conflict inside the building was more than just a physical manipulation of the space she occupied; it was a battle for her will. In admitting defeat, certain adjustments were made possible for Kizmet. Just as Shadow had some dominion of Space, Kizmet has a more limited but no less powerful dominion over the interaction of consciousness and time. What was a memory, after all, but a window into the past reality held by our consciousness? The frustrating endeavor, the peculiar building, all traces of the incident faded from her memory.

In the distance, hidden in the building's shade, Shadow emerged, a smirk playing on her lips. She looked around to be sure no other agent of The Demon was in the area. Satisfied, she stepped into the shadow at the side of the building, and in the blink of an eye, she was in Lady Fortuna's room. The two shared a knowing glance, signifying the success of their plan and the need to update the others.

CHAPTER 18

"WHAT A TANGLED WEB WE WEAVE..."

© SYNTHTOPIA #2140

Chapter Synopses: Warlock's Quantum Emitter. What strange, dark powers will this device unleash? The Zenith team must crack this mystery before it is too late.

The underground bunker was dimly lit, punctuated by the radiant amber glow emanating from the Warlock's Quantum Emitter. The object seemed both ancient and advanced, a juxtaposition that added a layer of intrigue to this already mysterious device. Its primitive appearance belied its capabilities; glowing tubes and inscriptions on its surface pulsed with life, giving it an otherworldly aura. Unfortunately, this was only a holographic replica constructed from the files that they were able to secure during the recent raid of Warlock's research.

Daedalus, with his sharp intellect and analytical prowess, along with Cipher, known for his unmatched decryption skills, were engrossed in the process of discovery.

According to the information retrieved from Warlock's secret files, they were able to reconstruct a portion of the Warlock's early research team's notes. Apparently, Warlock had gotten his hands on an ancient artifact that had some kind of housing similar to the one whose specs they had seized.

The journal stated that the scientists were subjecting the "proto emitter," as they called it, to every nondestructive test at their disposal. They had determined early on in their work that the emitter did not use any standard interfaces that they were familiar with. In fact, inexact dating of some of the components came back with carbon-14 age of many millennia in age, while others were clearly manufactured more recently. Those elements had clearly been of a custom fabrication and cutting-edge alloy assembly. The energies bound within the device were both off the charts and of barely detectable levels from one moment to the next, as if the energy profile was phasing across realities, and they could only perceive it for the brief periods when it existed in their realm.

They had finally been able to map a series of amplitude cycles and affix a carrier wave device to one of the junctions between very old and very new components to monitor flux within the device. They had thus made some progress towards understanding its potential and knew it was fundamentally designed with quantum effects in mind. They were still struggling to understand how to tap into that potential when the file data ended, thanks to the remote data erase program initiated by the Warlock.

Daedalus and Cipher pored over fragmented data, piece by piece, like a digital jigsaw collected from their many other operations. Their goal was to understand the depths of Warlock's ambition and the extent of his technological advancements. Unfortunately, they also had to admit that the files they had collected were only preliminary research and that much more advanced discoveries could already have been made.

With MEO's calculated guidance, they began to see patterns in the many different fragments. "This technology," Daedalus began, "it's a bridge. A bridge between quantum physics and... something older, perhaps spiritual."

Cipher raised an eyebrow, "The Spirit Realm? But how could Warlock possibly know about that? It's been hidden, a secret. If Warlock understood the implications of such a connection, he and his fellow Executive Team members would be waging an all-out war to eliminate or control access to it. Not to mention the fact that our operations would have been shut down long ago."

"That's what's unnerving," Daedalus continued, "This Quantum Emitter, despite its archaic exterior, is attempting to channel the same powers the Spirit Animals and the Shaman possess without really understanding their nature. It's like he's accidentally trying to recreate a bridge to the Spirit Realm as a byproduct of following the capabilities of the quantum potential underneath our universe, and he's getting dangerously close based on the notes we have seen. However, his researchers seem to think this is all purely a quantum mechanics tool. They do not seem to understand the connection to a deeper layer of reality, but what they DO get is dangerous enough."

As the pieces began to fall into place, the weight of their discovery became clear. Molusk Corp wasn't just trying to harness quantum technology; they aimed to control and weaponize the spiritual energies of the universe even though they still thought of them as "forces" that they could program and control.

MEO projected a hologram, showing the potential capabilities. "If Warlock succeeds, Molusk Corp could read the thoughts of individuals, manipulate matter on a quantum level, and even achieve teleportation. The implications are... catastrophic."

MEO proceeded to display a series of simulations of how SYNTHTOPIA might rapidly evolve under such conditions should Molusk Corp have the power he had described. Simulation after simulation rippled across the screen as if they were looking at a multitude of "timelines" play out at high speed of depressing dystopian destinies. Finally, MEO stopped. None of those outcomes looked like a place where they would want to live.

Looking at the data again, Daedalus commented, "Since they are only looking at this from a mechanical perspective rather than a merging of spirit and physical realities, their design will be inherently flawed. Entropic decay will find an expression somewhere in their design. We just cannot predict the where and how until we know more. Unfortunately, if they were able to get this far, they have the potential for a world-ending failure under the right conditions."

The realization sent a shiver down Cipher's spine. "And if this is only half the project, what horrors does 'Tartarus' contain?" he whispered, the name of Warlord's secret lab sending chills through the room.

Daedalus clenched his fist. "We need to find that lab before it's too late. Before, the balance between the spiritual and the physical is forever altered by Molusk or some other corporate that might get their hands on these secrets. We have the potential to become more, but they have the potential to destroy everything."

The three, bound by a shared purpose, knew that time was of the essence. While the Molusk Corp was weaving their dangerous web, Daedalus, Cipher, and MEO had to untangle it and safeguard the realm from impending doom. They would find that lab!

CHAPTER 19

"SECRETS TAKEN TO THE RAVE"

© SYNTHTOPIA #1665

Chapter Synopses: DJ Gurl, Street name, Digi. For her, music is life. Warlock's entertainment frequencies are both addictive and repress free thought, but Digi knows how to counter those frequencies and works with the Destabilizers by supporting the floating raves that citizens go to under the radar from central view. Even more importantly, Cipher helps her inject her music streams into the very broadcasts that Warlock is using to control the minds of the citizens. How long can she keep this up?

The dark alleys and twisting streets echoed with a pulsating beat. The city, blanketed by the oppressive frequencies of Warlock's broadcasts, seemed to breathe a sigh of relief in certain corners where the light of resistance thrived. One such corner was where DJ Gurl, or "Digi" as the streets knew her, held her clandestine raves. Places that were both chaotic and calming. The free energy from her sets was uplifting rather than a brutal assault on the senses. Even though people danced and *moved* to external beats or internal rhythms, they knew, somehow, that it was THEIR expression of freedom rather than one imposed on them by Digi or anyone else. They would leave tired but at peace and able to resist Warlock's broadcasts for a time.

Walking into the dimly lit, sprawling underground venue, Eve felt the atmosphere change. The pressure that had been building inside her head, a byproduct of Warlock's pervasive frequencies being broadcast throughout the city, began to subside. The vibrant glow of neon lights painted the dance floor, and the crowd moved as one, united by the hypnotic beats spun by Digi, but each with an individuality all their own.

Artemis, her eyes closed, swayed to the music, lost in its enchanting embrace. She had been the one to introduce Eve to these raves, these pockets of freedom amidst the suffocating control. Eve walked up to her, and without opening her eyes, Artemis smiled and said loudly, "Glad you could make it." Eve had to smile back. In the midst of the crowd, Eve could feel a cocoon of sounds and vibrations being woven around her. The lights balance with the music to work their magic. Just as she was relaxing into the moment, knowing she would have to wait to talk to Digi anyway, there was a disturbance in the air.

A group of factory workers had come in together, and they were clearly looking for a fight to blow off some steam. Their angry energy was at odds with the musical balm around them. Artemis opened her eyes and gave a brief frown. She immediately moved toward the men, her silvery hair and dress weaving through the crowd and giving Eve the strange impression of moonlight twinkling through the leaves of a forest. Shaking her head, she followed, ready to assist with her biosynth reflexes if needed.

One of the biggest men in the group looked at Artemis as she approached, and his aggression shifted into a different mode. One that Eve did not like at all. "Here we go," She thought to herself.

Artemis walked up and stood in front of him. She looked from him to his crew while he made the obvious perusal of her form and whistled. Eve almost rolled her eyes, almost. There was too much tension to not take this seriously. Eve was about to step forward when Artemis signaled with her hand out of sight behind her back for Eve to stay put. Taking the hint, Eve let Artemis, the "Moon Maiden," have the spotlight.

"Well, well," The leader said in a rather unoriginal line, "What a pretty little shiny for me and my boys to play with," clearly expecting the threat to scare the luminescent flower in front of him. Eve looked over at the "boys" in question. They were smirking as she had expected, but she noticed that the tension had gone out of a couple of the men, and they were leaning on the bar now. One had started to order a drink.

Artemis looked at the big guy and, surprising both him and Eve, smiled brightly. On her, that is the only description that worked. She could simply be radiant with her smile. She said, "Hello there, you big strong man! Have you come to rescue me from the boredom here? Just <u>listen</u> to the music they are playing. Go ahead and simply <u>look</u> at the light show. No, don't just sample the noise or glance at the lights. You need to <u>listen</u> to how *calm* and boring things are."

Eve was noticing the inflections in Artemis' voice and the way the tension was leaving more of the crew. They were starting to relax but the big guy was not having any of it.

"I can take care of your boredom, Lady," he said, stepping forward aggressively, "but first, you are going to learn not to tell me what to do! You are going to learn to do what I tell **you** to do and like it!"

As he went to grab her neck and dominate her, Artemis struck with the speed of an arrow in the moonlight. With the big man's body blocking her moves from the rest of the crew, who probably knew what was coming and simply had lost their focus to the lights and music by now, she stepped inside his reach rather than cringing away as he expected. Her right hand grabbed his arm just behind the ulnar nerve while her left hand snaked forward and up with her index finger and thumb, forming an arc that crashed into his throat with a "slap" of force. If she had used her knuckles with that strike, Eve observed, she probably would have crushed his larynx and killed him. As it was, he immediately collapsed, choking, and brought his hands to his throat.

She motioned to two of his crew who had looked over concerned. "Please buy him a drink for me when he recovers," she said, "and remind him that the hunter can very easily become the prey. Oh, and maybe he will listen to the music and relax if YOU tell him to."

With that, she led Eve back to the floor, where they enjoyed the rest of Digi's set. On the way back to the dance floor, Eve reminded herself that the Moon Maiden was also a huntress and a great dance partner.

As the last beat of the set faded away, Digi removed her headphones and stepped off the platform, making her way through the crowd of admirers to meet up with Eve and Artemis.

"You feel it, don't you?" Digi said, her voice just above a whisper. "The release, the freedom."

Eve nodded, "It's like a weight being lifted. But how?"

Digi smirked, "It's all about the frequencies. Warlock uses them to spread panic, fear, and compliance. They ride on light and sound waves throughout the city, softening minds for his more direct programming. But with the right counter-frequencies," she tapped her custom mixer, "you can break the spell. With the right music, you can also inspire the potential inside each person, at least for a time."

Eve eyed the intricate mixer, noting symbols that eerily resembled those used by the Spirit Animals. "How did you come by this?"

Digi winked, "A secret best kept between me and the Spirit Animals. All you need to know is that it's our weapon against Warlock. With Cipher's help, I've been streaming my sets right into Warlock's broadcasts. A little *sonic alchemy* to counteract his *malevolent magic*." She smiled at her own wordplay.

But even amidst the hope and defiance, Eve could see the exhaustion in Digi's eyes. "How long can you keep this up?" she asked, concerned.

"As long as it takes," Digi responded with determination and nodding to the factory workers still relaxing by the bar despite the almost altercation that happened and letting them know that she was aware of the damage control Artemis had done. "But tonight, I could use a break."

Together, the three left the rave's pulsating heart as a new DJ took the stage, albeit with less of a calming effect than Digi produced but a great set of music in any case, winding their way through the city to visit a familiar face. They were going to visit The Inventor. Tonight, as the music of freedom continued to echo in the distance, new plans and strategies would be forged in the fight against the darkness.

CHAPTER 20

"SONIC ALCHEMY"

Chapter Synopses: DJ Gurl's Mixer. Another artifact imbued with Spirit. Digi is able to counter the effects of the mind-controlling broadcasts from the Warlock. While his reach extends across the whole city, Digi can protect the area around her. How can she push the tide back even further? Perhaps The Inventor can help her?

The room was once again awash in a radiant neon glow. Everywhere one looked, arrays of colorful lights danced, creating an atmosphere that felt almost magical. The heart of this luminous display was DJ Gurl's mixer, its dials and switches casting reflections that painted the walls with a rhythmic play of lights.

Daedalus examined the equipment with a mix of fascination and respect. Beside the massive mixer was its much smaller counterpart—a device that could fit in the palm of a hand or be concealed inside of a pocket, that held the promise of turning the tide in their fight against Warlock. In honor of the mixer and DG Gurl's description of her effect on Warlock's negative influence, they called the artifact "Sonic Alchemy."

"Remarkable," Daedalus murmured, running his fingers over the smaller device's sleek surface. "It's hard to believe we've managed to condense the capabilities of your mixer into this much smaller form factor."

DJ Gurl grinned, her eyes gleaming with pride. "With your expertise and my knowledge of sound, it was only a matter of time." After a pause, she looked over at The Electron Cat, MEO, and sighed, "Of course, our most enigmatic ally was almost a big help."

MEO did not rise to the passive-aggressive behavior. Really, not a smart tactic to try on any cat. After a moment, however, he relented and said, 'You know I have been instructed by the great Tigris Icarus to hold certain information back until you attain further levels of enlightenment. The knowledge is too dangerous. I shared what I could, and you figured the rest out."

Digi noted the somewhat defensive tone from MEO as well as the very formal title he used for their ally, Electra. She knew Electra was the leader of the Spirit Animals, but she was far less clear on their exact hierarchy. All of their allies seemed to have a particular domain of power and influence except Electra. MEO had amazing abilities within the Spirit network and mundane digital domains that greatly enhanced the efforts of The Inventor (devices), The Engineer (robotics, spirit networks, and synths), and Cyber Bull/Cyber Bill (logistics, pattern trends).

Clearly, he was a tireless ally, and she knew he was helping as far as he was allowed. That deference, however, made it seem that he really was just a cat in the shadow of the tigress form that Electra manifested to them. Even the enigmatic Shadow, who seemed to control space and items in the physical realm, had limits. However, now that she thought about it, her affinity to Lady Fortuna (with her Future affinity) and The Digital Monk (Atemiwaza- with his superhuman grounding in the Present) made more sense to her all of a sudden. Electra, on the other hand, seemed to have no limits. She seemed to have a bottomless well of power and knowledge. Even knowing that such a conclusion was flawed (it MUST be flawed, right?), she decided to give MEO a break.

"I know you did, MEO," she said with absolute sincerity. "You are a constant friend and ally, and we appreciate everything that you do for us."

MEO, feeling somewhat mollified and more than a little grateful for Digi's sensitivity, gave a simple, almost regal nod of acceptance and the slow blink of affection that they had all come to understand.

Eve, who had been silently observing the duo, asked, "So this... small artifact can disrupt Warlock's devices?"

Daedalus nodded. "In theory, it should counteract the effects of his devices of influence, persuasion, and illusion. We've even added modifications and booster elements with the potential to disrupt the Quantum Emitter's capabilities, the weaker ones at least." That last bit was said with a well-deserved sense of pride. It had taken them quite a bit of reverse engineering from incomplete schematics, but with the addition of some of the spirit tech he had been developing, they had made something unique.

DJ Gurl added, "But it's not just about disruption. We want to send out our own frequencies, our own messages, to liberate the minds under Warlock's control." She never lost sight of her particular mission. She had lost someone once to the kind of despair that was the occasional side effect of Warlock's broadcasts, and she had sworn to fight it. Warlock had taken his knowledge of the human psyche and turned it into a weapon. Well, it made him the embodiment of Digi's fight, and she was sure he had no idea what kind of enemy he had made. He would learn.

As she contemplated the irony and the need for her unwavering campaign against Warlock, there was a moment of contemplative silence among the group as a whole. Then Eve broke in with a question that weighed on all their minds. "So....How do we deploy it?"

Daedalus sighed, "That's the challenge. In a general sense, just having Sonic Alchemy on you will create a sphere of protection, but more advanced uses will need additional equipment. If your will is trained enough, it should empower the capabilities of MEO or someone like Atemiwaza. Once the current situation is resolved, Digi will be able to work with Cipher and Shadow on infiltration plans that get them to key broadcast points where they can use Warlock's own transmissions as carrier waves. While we have noted some modifications after we crashed his party, I have not noted anything advanced enough to deliver adaptive countermeasures on the fly."

Well into his vision of the systems held by their adversary, The Inventor continued, "Without multiple, advanced AI installations all throughout the edge of their networks and physical locations, they simply would not be resilient enough to stop us. Such an architecture would effectively require them to embrace a decentralized protocol rather than their centralized control. This, in turn, would require an organizational restructuring into an increasingly trustless and open infrastructure. They are not culturally, psychologically, or technologically able to do this. The irony is that if they did make the necessary changes to fight us effectively, we would have already won a major battle against the tyranny of the centralized autocracy!"

Realizing that he had gotten caught up in his review of their circumstances, Daedalus went back to the question at hand. "In order to move on to the broadcasting mission," he said, "We need to find Tartarus. Whatever is taking place, there is potentially a serious threat, AND it may be the only place with an energy signature strong enough to boost the mini-mixer's signals throughout the city. This would allow us to override Warlock's signal everywhere all at once rather than in a series of dangerous missions."

DJ Gurl's eyes narrowed in determination. "Then we'll find it. With this device, we have the element of surprise. Warlock won't know what hit him."

The stakes were higher than ever. With the power of Sonic Alchemy at their fingertips, the group was ready to embark on to the next part of their quest!

CHAPTER 21

"IN THE NICK OF TIME"

Chapter Synopses: Dark Storm. Street name, Nimbus (or Nick). He is tied into the Bounty Hunters and often works at cross purposes with The Demon. Dark Storm, as his name and appearance suggest, is a loner with a strong sense of independence and justice. He likes to be in the middle of the action and seeks to curb the growing overreach of powers by some factions in the Bounty department.

The neon streets were a quiet hum, an ambiance that Eve had grown to appreciate. The soft drizzle that had begun earlier painted everything in a reflective sheen, allowing the lights to play in brilliant, scattered patterns. As she made her way back to Lady Fortuna's apartments to update her on the Sonic Alchemy artifact and, with the team's urging, seek a reading on where they could use the device, she felt a tug of unease. Something felt off, but she couldn't pinpoint it. Perhaps if she had more time to practice the exercises that The Digital Monk had given her or even more experience in reading the signals from her Light energy with her enhanced awareness since her encounter with Nitro, she would have been able to prepare herself. Perhaps. In this case, however, she was not prepared at all.

Lost in her thoughts and encouraged by her earlier interactions with the team, she failed to notice the lurking shadow that silently followed her.

The Demon was known for her cunning and tenacity. She had a knack for tracking, and Banshee's mysterious activities hadn't escaped her attention. The disappearing data on the building (which had initially shown as a hole in the city schematics before fading entirely into a false mesh of newly formed drawings) and the vague report from Banshee had stoked her suspicions, and she had decided to see for herself what was going on.

As it had many, many times before in her life, her instinct was correct. Just as she was committing the building measurements to an immutable record and intended to store it in a specially shielded box Warlock had given her (and only her, but she was not aware of that detail), she spotted Eve. Just like her Hunter earlier, Eve triggered several red flags and presented them on her HUD dashboard as a low-level miscreant with likely ties to more important collaborators.

Unlike her Hunter, the Demon was quick to spot that Eve was an advanced biosynth. Further, there were strange energy signatures she emitted that fuzzed her screens. Again, unlike her minion, The Demon knew what caused this kind of effect. She and Nitro both did the same thing. Eve was Touched. Based on her affiliations, it was likely that she was of the Light variety. Interesting.

Suddenly, a puzzle piece clicked into place for The Demon. She *knew* something had been off with Nitro's report from his "incident" at Warlords distribution center. She had dismissed it as some form of tampering on his part as a move in the power games that the Executive Team played amongst themselves since he had nothing else to gain from such action until now. Clearly, he had failed on multiple levels and tried to cover it up!

1. He failed to intercept whatever had brought the Collaborators and/or Destabilizers together for the meeting.
2. He had allowed himself to be led into a trap and captured (not killed, captured)
3. He had come face to face with a Light Touched and let her live.

With her reactions bleeding from scorn to humor to disgust as she went through her checklist of Nitro's failures, she returned her attention to the figure moving quickly up the side of the street to the unmarked building and carrying an object that was clearly, to her, precious cargo. Eve's biosynth nature, her hurried pace, and the evident urgency she showed while clutching a package decided it for The Demon. This was the perfect time to strike. Seeking to subdue and interrogate, The Demon eschewed energy weapons and triggered a telescoping electrified baton to extend and drop into her grip from a slot on the inside of her armor that looked to the world as if it was a vambrace from the armor of an ancient warrior. As soon as the baton scanned her palm signature, it energized to a very high but not quite lethal setting. It was the default setting for the Demon.

However, as she launched forward, a gunshot rang out. The bullet missed, kicking up a cement piece of shrapnel from the sidewalk, but forced the Demon to swerve, revealing Dark Storm, who went by Nimbus on the bounty roster or Nick, as some of his friends knew him, coming at her with guns blazing.

Nick's rapid response had caught The Demon off guard. He had been observing from the shadows, recognizing the Demon's Hunter's unusual activities and foreseeing a possible confrontation. Being allies with the Red Knight in the Bounty sector had its perks, and one of them was knowing who the players were and being adept at reading situations before they boiled over.

"Back off!" Nick yelled, lunging at The Demon, his coat flaring out behind him like the wings of some avian predator. His guns had disappeared, and he was wielding twin batons of his own with "sonic hammer" tips. He knew that The Demon's electro-graphene armor would shed high-velocity kinetic projectiles, and he worried about collateral damage, perhaps even to Eve. So, he had switched to his batons. While he held either the main grip or the side handle (allowing the baton to swing in arcs or to reinforce the forearm or support a punch with the main grip), the tips would be active. If he released the grips to hold the weapon by the end to use the other ends in various joint lock patterns or as a hammer or thrusting weapon, the tips deactivated. Their versatility was why Nick preferred them, and they fit his street brawler style perfectly.

The Demon, taken aback by the intervention, retaliated with fierce but poorly coordinated blows. Sparks flew as their weapons clashed, filling the air with a cacophony of metallic sounds. While Nick was a veteran of many one-on-one fights, The Demon was a synth and had a gift for betrayal in all its forms. That included fighting. She would deliver perfectly executed feints and shift attacks to a pivot that struck off-center on Nick but in mostly unprotected areas. If his armor had been less complete, his reflexes would be below his best, and frankly, if he had not sparred extensively with Atemiwaza, who was naturally familiar with Drunken Boxing style (as he called it) that was very similar in style to the off-balance attacks The Demon was using, Nick would have been lost in the initial counterattack from The Demon.

Fortunately, he HAD formed strategies to counter her deceptions and was able to land several strikes in succession with the tips of his batons. Unlike a bullet or hard impact that her armor could deflect, an electric attack that she could ground, or even a laser attack that could be diffracted, the sonic tips sent impulse energy *through* her armor to be absorbed by her softer fibers. In other words, those strikes HURT! Worse, the frequency of the sonic shockwaves seemed designed to disrupt the signals through her synthetic tissues and degrade her performance. It would not be noticeable for simple tasks like running or walking, but for a combat sequence, it lowered her performance to an unacceptable level.

The Demon tried, once again, to resort to betrayal. Making several feints that appeared to strike in one direction with an intent to pivot to another threat angle but really designed to maneuver around Nick to get at Eve, who was staring in seeming panic at the viciousness of the conflict, The Demon prepared herself to make a grab. Possibly sensing the Dark in the Demon, Eve moved quickly behind Nick. Realizing what had almost happened, Nick took a deep breath and prepared to escalate the conflict further rather than expose Eve to continued danger.

However, realizing she was outmatched and without the element of surprise, The Demon decided to cut her losses. In a whirlwind of motion, she threw a smoke bomb, shrouding the area in a thick, impenetrable haze. This high-tech smoke bomb also disrupted various scanning methods such that the gear in Nick's helmet was useless. Sensing further deceit, he backed away and prepared to shield Eve from attacks emerging from the cloud. When the smoke cleared, The Demon was gone.

Nick, panting heavily, approached Eve. "You alright?" he gasped out.

Eve nodded, still in shock. "Yes, thanks to you. But who was she?"

Nick sighed, holstering his batons. "That's a conversation for another time. For now, she is **not** a friend. Let's get you to safety first; we can talk there."

And with that, the two of them disappeared into the neon-lit streets, their silhouettes blending into the city's rhythm, each harboring secrets and untold stories. Behind them, in the street, the immutable storage crystal lay in pieces on the ground. A silent victim of the fierce battle. Before dawn, automated street cleaners would move through, and the only memory of the battle would be the chip in the sidewalk from Nick's warning shot.

CHAPTER 22

"DEAD MAN'S HAND"

© SYNTHTOPIA #2087

Chapter Synopses: Dead Man's Hand, An ominous vision given to Lady Fortuna. When Death deals your hand, your only choice is to play it like your life depends on it!

The labyrinthine corridors leading to Kizmet's sanctum echoed with a low hum, a juxtaposition of the outside world's chaotic rhythm. Nick's presence was a reassuring anchor for Eve as they wound their way towards the spiritual seer.

Upon entering, the room was bathed in a cerulean glow, casting eerie, dancing shadows. Candles flickered, their flames mirroring Kizmet's heightened energies. Eve could tell that something significant had happened in her absence, but Kizmet did not give her time to ask for an explanation. Without preamble, she beckoned Eve forward and began a ritual far more profound than their last encounter. Chanting in an ancient tongue, her eyes rolled back, revealing the milky whites.

Eve was nervous. This was not how their last meeting went. Other than Kizmet being prepared for their visit, she seemed to be an almost different person. In fact, she thought, it was as if she and Dark Storm had left one field of battle only to step into the middle of another. Unlike the recent altercation in the street, however, this was a battleground that neither of them was familiar with.

Time seemed to stretch and contract, reality blurring. The room grew colder, the atmosphere dense with the weight of potentiality.

Unseen by her two guests, Kizmet *Travelled*. She pushed her sharpened will through the quantum foam of the universe to the Nexus of "Everywhen." She had been here many times, of course, but each journey was fraught with fresh peril. There was no "backwards" or "forwards" in this place. She knew which direction had more flexible probabilities than others. She considered this to be more of an upstream and downstream with respect to the cascade of probabilities in this framework of what might be.

With an infinite number of choices, she was also required to anchor her awareness so she did not drift free and become lost in the fabric of the universe. She often wondered if that was how some Spirit entities came to exist, but she was never sure how to broach the subject with Electra. Shadow had told her that the Spirit Tiger was very wise and had access to ancient knowledge but that she would only share with those who were ready.

Kizmet had heard that each Traveler in this place had a personalized mechanism that they used for their anchor. For some, it was a thread spooled from the core of their being and rewound on the return trip. Others trailed breadcrumbs or planted mushrooms, or… the list, like this place, was endless. The point was that for each anchor, there was a danger that increased over "time" (duration of the visit) and "distance" (how far upstream or downstream) one traveled. Downstream was always more dangerous. Sharp crystals could emerge from the grounds to slowly cut the thread. One bird and then another might appear to eat the breadcrumbs. A blight could slowly spread across the mushrooms. Whatever the manifestation, the danger was present on every trip.

In this case, Kizmet moved quickly through the Nexus as she felt a pull to a collapsing set of probable futures. She had never witnessed anything like this big a probability event horizon. There was no path she could see around the blackness. It was as if all paths bent inward to end at this destination. As she became "nearer" to the inky blackness, she felt as if there was an awareness inside that was sensing her intrusion into its potential reality. Unbelievably, that awareness appeared to be reaching out to her with its will from this future place. Questing for the entity that dared spy on it from afar.

Kizmet had seen enough; as she raced back along her path, she maintained her discipline in order to avoid false anchors, false "Kizmet homes" of *almost her,* and returned to her mind. In the gestalt of awareness of "the Past" and "now Future," an image imprinted itself on her occult sight, The Dead Man's Hand.

Meanwhile, Back in the room

Hours felt like minutes, and then, with a sharp gasp, Kizmet emerged from her trance.

"What did you see?" Eve questioned, anxiety evident in her voice.

Kizmet's face was pale, her countenance troubled. "The Dead Man's Hand," she whispered absently, the weight of her vision apparent to her visitors.

Nick frowned. "Isn't that just a legend?" he asked. Then, after a pause, "What does it mean?"

Kizmet shook her head. "It is very real. It's an omen. A warning of a calamity that will befall not just the Destabilizers and Collaborators but the entire city and beyond. Our fate dangles on the precipice."

Eve felt her chill deepen. If someone with as much experience as Lady Fortuna was this shaken, she knew that things were serious indeed. "How do we prevent this?" she asked.

Kizmet took a deep breath. "Tartarus. Warlord's secret lab. We must find it because it is a key. But..." her voice wavered, "I cannot guide you any further, nor can I see your victory. There are forces at play, converging in the future, that cloud the quantum pathways I tap into. If I force my way through again, they might see me, see us."

They all paused at this news, unsure of how to even begin to respond. Then, Nick clenched his fist, determination lighting his features. "We'll find another way."

With a resolute nod, he turned to Eve, ensuring she was ready for the journey ahead. "You need to be careful. Try to keep a low profile for a while. I will go muster some assistance from my friends in the bounty trade, the ones I know we can trust. Why not head back to HQ and debrief the rest of the team."

And then, with a final look at Kizmet, he dashed out, seeking his bounty hunter allies, the Red Knight, known as Samurai or Sam, and Ace, the sharp-eyed Diana. If anyone could unearth hidden secrets, it would be them.

As Eve watched him leave, she clutched the package closer, realizing the gravity of their mission. The fate of the city rested in their hands, and the game had only just begun.

CHAPTER 23

"OK, WHO'S PICKING UP THE BILL?"

© SYNTHTOPIA #1311

Chapter Synopses: Cyber Bill, One of the three known as Cyber Bull, Cyber Bill, and Mecha Bull (their AI/transport in the background). Street Names, CeeBee, Bill, and Embee. Bill was able to show CeeBee how to look beyond the economic illusions that the Cyber Bulls had been enthralled by. Together, they make a powerful, if unusual, group.

The neon lights of the headquarters cast a dim, futuristic glow on the assembled team as Eve burst in. The mood was tense. She placed the Sonic Alchemy device on the table, its contours and intricate details drawing everyone's attention. She took advantage of the pause to launch into a retelling of the recent events she had experienced.

She took everyone through her visits with Digi, Lady Fortuna, and Nimbus, as well as the dire news of the Dead Man's Hand. Some of her stories were known to some of those present, but now everyone knew everything she did. She is aware that it was a lot to absorb and that the concern of a force so powerful that the Past needed to fear it reaching back from the Future, well, that was simply unprecedented.

The room fell silent for a moment, the weight of their mission pressing down on them all.

But it wasn't long before the room erupted into a cacophony of voices. Suggestions, concerns, and questions filled the air, and each team member tried to process the new information and form a plan of action.

Several team members who had not been part of the previous events had to get up to speed quickly, so they had an air of panic as they tried to make sense of everything. Others seemed calm but were no less frantic in their attempts to devise a plan.

In the midst of this turmoil, a calm voice rose above the rest. It was Bill, his cybernetic hornlike enhancements subtly gleaming under the dim lights. "Hold on, now!" he said, clearing his throat for emphasis.

The room quietened, all eyes on him.

"CeeBee and I have already worked on decrypting Warlord's moves in his regular businesses. He leaves traces, patterns, and digital footprints. We just need to scale up our efforts so we can get a larger picture of his total operations. I know Eve mentioned that Warlord had "off-the-books" activities when she first joined us. Those leave trails too. A lab like Tartarus can't operate in a vacuum. Our earlier run-in showed that he is a superior strategist when he controls the field of battle. He prefers economic and logistical maneuvers as they tend to be less wasteful, and he is running a business after all."

Eve nodded in agreement. "Exactly. And the resources used in the lab have to be transported from somewhere. If we track the supply chain across both official and unofficial delivery channels, we can find its location."

Ripples of agreement spread across the room. With Bill's approach in mind, the previously chaotic scene now seemed to have a clearer direction. Each team member dove into their tasks, drawing on their individual strengths. Several teams conferred with Bill on potential data sources they could secure. Another offered access to a new viral matrix mainframe that could be enhanced by some of the Inventor tools, the Engineer's access to the Spirit network, and support from MEO.

Then, the teams either went out on their errands or coalesced into work teams around the room. As the room buzzed with activity, Bill remained near the entrance, his stance relaxed but alert.

"Bill," one of the team members asked curiously, "aren't you going to help with the planning?"

Without turning his head, Bill replied with a hint of amusement in his voice, "Just waiting for a ride."

In reality, Bill had been in a three-way triumvirate that connected Embee, CeeBee, and himself via their respective horn-like implants. These were sophisticated phased array transceivers that allowed them low latency, high bandwidth, and secure communications, as well as a shared virtual workspace. While heavy processing needed to be done outside of the space, they could still manipulate layered, three-dimensional data schemas in the workspace with ease. These could then be processed in an overlay of physical routes, resources, topographical maps, and so much more. This was where the three team members could look at a cojoined cyber/real space and spot anomalies. They may not have the raw processing power of a synth, but their combined capabilities allowed for intuitive and exponential progress that often exceeded that of a synth and delivered insights in seconds that would not occur to a synth in years. For raw data processing, however, they needed offline help.

"Well, "Bill thought to himself, "Help was on the way!"

The sound of heavy machinery grew louder, and soon, the formidable figure of Mecha Bull or "Embee" came into view, illuminating the entrance with its brilliant lights. The majestic transport machine stood ready to aid in their mission, reinforcing the team's determination to succeed. Without breaking their three-way connection, Bill sauntered up the ramp into the belly of the beast.

CHAPTER 24

"THE RUNNING OF THE BULLS"

© SYNTHTOPIA #1310

Chapter Synopses: Cyber Bull, One of the three known as Cyber Bull, Cyber Bill, and Mecha Bull (their transport). Street Names, CeeBee, Bill, and Embee. Bill was able to show CeeBee how to look beyond the economic illusions that the Cyber Bulls had been enthralled by. Once he sets his mind to a problem, you do not want to get in his way!

Rain trickled down the neon-lit streets as Bill leaned against a building, lost in thought while he waited again for CeeBee to return from a visit with his "contact." The subtle hum of the cyber city resonated with the memories of his first encounter with CeeBee. A mammoth figure with sharp horns, metallic sheen, and an aura that demanded respect. At first glance, CeeBee was the epitome of aggression, a being conditioned to power and dominance.

Their initial meetings were fraught with tension. Bill, ever the diplomat, had approached CeeBee to discuss a trade agreement. The Collaborators operated under several business umbrellas and had to show normal commercial activity or risk discovery. Bill, it seemed, had a talent for negotiating with Corporations and their procurement teams, as well as seeing through deal structures that seemed to benefit his side of an agreement but hurt the returns over time.

The discussions were lengthy, intense, and often heated. Bill knew that some of this was an act, just another negotiating tool. As the negotiations progressed, Bill began to see past the Cyber Bull's metallic exterior. He realized that beneath that tough facade was a being who was fundamentally good.

Like any good negotiator, Bill could "seat himself on the other side of the table," as the saying went. When he did so now, he realized that CeeBee's perspective was not rooted in malevolence, but in conditioning. Bill had known some of this, but his past associations with Bulls had led him to believe that they were willing participants in the charade. Based on the data that CeeBee had shown him in an attempt to win back 23 basis points (0.23%) on their last contract line, Bill realized that he had been wrong. They really had no idea of the truth.

Molusk Corp had spun an intricate web of economic deceit, convincing the Cyber Bulls of a skewed reality. Through methodical discussions, Bill illuminated the truth for CeeBee: the profits promised by Molusk Corp were but illusions. Their indirect control over the money supply rendered the bulls' earnings nonexistent. Molusk manipulated supply, demand, productivity, prices, and even the relative value of the medium of exchange. In real terms, they gained nothing. Assets went up, costs went up, and – in nominal terms – profits went up. When looked at in REAL terms, i.e., what can money buy you, they stayed in the same place. They were left treading water while the Corp – with the assets (buildings, mines, land, metals, farms, etc) – got wealthier. Oh, they did cut some of the Bulls in on a share of the Corp profits but only reluctantly and if the Bull had unusual leverage. The rest of the population were the ones to really suffer from an invisible tax. The rich get richer, and the poor get poorer, yes. The Corps, however, also got more POWER!

Bill introduced the disillusioned CeeBee to the Destabilizers' decentralized financial system, revealing the true essence of wealth. It was a radical shift for the Cyber Bull. The realization was both enlightening and shattering. It was clear to CeeBee that the rest of the Bulls weren't ready for this truth, but he would not let that stand in the way of his progress.

Instead of retreating, CeeBee joined Bill and Embee, the AI-powered Mecha Bull, and they… collaborated. They became an inside link to the Destabilizers, navigating the treacherous waters of Molusk Corp's deception. But something more profound was happening to CeeBee.

As they continued their undercover operations, Sonic Wage, the Virtual Shaman, took CeeBee under his wing. He guided the Cyber Bull on a journey of self-discovery. The relentless urban chaos of the cyber world faded as CeeBee ventured deeper into the realms of his ancestral spirit. With Sonic Wage's mentorship, CeeBee began rekindling the essence of his true animal spirit. The raw, wild energy of the bull began to harmonize with the cybernetic advancements, creating a perfect amalgamation of nature and technology. CeeBee knew that it would be a very long time, if ever before, he would be able to harness Spirit in the manner of MEO or Shadow, but he felt the stirring of his gift. Partially, it would be an exponential growth of the patterning ability he now shared with Bill and Embee, but another part, he knew, would be an ability to inspire other Bulls. He would be an Alpha Bull, and when the time came, he knew that he would lead them in a Bull Run that would level the corporations that tried to pen them in.

Yes, the *Running of the Bulls* would be a beautiful time. In the meantime, he would help his friends, and the people who had been tricked like he and his kind were tricked. They deserved to be free too.

Bill watched CeeBee with pride. The Cyber Bull's transformation was a beacon of hope. If one could break free from the chains of conditioning in such a magnificent way, perhaps others could too. The battle against Molusk Corp was far from over, but with allies like CeeBee and Embee, the path ahead seemed a little brighter.

For now, the trio knew the task at hand. The future of the SYNTHTOPIA depended on their next moves, and they were ready to run headfirst to lock horns with the challenge.

CHAPTER 25

"WHEN IN DOUBT, FOLLOW THE MONEY"

© SYNTHTOPIA #2052

Chapter Synopses: Decentralization Node (Bitcoin Portal) used for access to monetary value, information, and identity storage and transfer outside of the central systems controlled by the megacorps. Central authority got tired of trying to shut it down and simply blocked access, or so they thought.

The vast neon cityscape loomed ahead, a beacon of intricacy and chaos, of connectivity and isolation. Dominating the view was a glowing Bitcoin Portal (now acting as a decentralization hub of Node for the Destabilizers), its radiance stark against the urban shadows. The Decentralization Node pulsated with a life of its own, a nexus where the digital world intersected with spiritual realms.

Nitro stood a few meters away, concealed in the rain-soaked alleyways. His frustration was palpable, manifesting as a smoky haze around his nimble figure. Usually, he was able to completely mask his presence and contain his energy, but ever since his run-in with the synth in the storage area, his dark energy swirled around inside him and escaped when he was particularly agitated.

Banshee's betrayal had been evident to him. A minuscule shift in demeanor that screamed treachery to Nitro's trained senses, and he knew who the master of treachery and betrayal in their group was. The Demon. Yet, The Demon remained elusive, always a step ahead, an enigma disappearing in the maze-like streets whenever he sought to follow her. He did not know that she could sense his Dark energy, a twin to her own, and use that sense to evade him.

He replayed the incident in the storage area over again in his mind, the feeling of being trapped, the knowledge that something impossible had just happened, leaving the smell of ozone in the cold, metallic air. His shock when he confirmed that the trail went cold, as if his quarry had simply vanished from the dead end by magic. Most vivid were the haunting eyes that locked onto his as the doors slammed shut. Those eyes, a mixture of defiance and sorrow, had imprinted on his soul, appearing in his restless dreams, urging him to seek their owner.

He had decided to retrace his steps from that night at the café and see if he could uncover any additional clues. Certainly, there were too many people NOT to leave some kind of trace. After all, they were merely human, and humans were sloppy. The path from the café to the storage area was unnaturally clean. That mysterious hacker must have covered their tracks. It did not matter if he investigated the firmware, offline storage, or active mem pools of any device that could have captured some portion of the electromagnetic spectrum, nothing.

Correction, nothing unusual. THAT was **something**. Normally, an intruder would simply wipe the data needed to cover their tracks. The tracks would be gone, but the wiped trail would be there. This hacker, or whoever was responsible, was able to actively edit out the trail while leaving a full content load. Put another way, it was as if the attacker had run a city area-sized full-scale simulation in parallel with real events, but without the things they did not want to be recorded, and fed the false reality into ALL the devices in the area. That was *very* unusual.

Nitro had several gifts with respect to surveillance equipment. That was how he edited the storage facility incident out of the logistics center memory and torpedoed the local AI in such a way that it looked like a malfunction. That had taken him almost an hour to crawl through the data streams and rewrite the necessary 7 minutes of live footage from a limited set of units in an environment where he had full access. Warlord would not be pleased to learn Nitro had gotten access long ago.

So, given the exponentially harder challenge of processing parallel reality and accessing all these devices nearly instantly meant that the hacker was not alone; they had massive processing capacity and a parallel network that could hit broad range device access without leaving footprints or triggering alarms. Leaving off the cold trail, he worked backwards to the café. Based on the clean payment record, he knew nothing was there, BUT he tried to backtrace payments.

As he suspected, the payment was made from a decentralized payment system. While he knew he could not trace the source, he DID find the IP address of the last node from which the payment confirmation came. He tried to hack the Bitcoin Portal interface with his advanced attack programs, but it was like trying to grab hold of a ball of oil. Simply, there is no structure to grab. Shielded and protected code was run in cyberspace with obfuscated elements randomly circulating across multiple active portals. What struck him, however, was the vast quantity of information being transferred. He had always only looked at the monetary volume, which was nothing compared to the mainstream financial system, but he had never bothered to look at the rest.

One header record that acted as a portal identifier used a strange term: Decentralization Node. He also recognized an authentication challenge format. It matched a biosynth token that he had seized on one of his missions. He never turned it in and wanted to study it to see if he could use it to his advantage against the War Twins as they jockeyed for position under the unrelenting gaze of Tyrannus.

It was evident to Nitro that he had been overlooking a fundamental piece in this vast jigsaw. He had underestimated the role of Decentralization Nodes in this new world. Perhaps the biosynth tokens had revitalized them, or perhaps they had always been more than they appeared. He had no way of knowing.

He did not yet know that they did this by creating bridges between the tangible infrastructure and the ethereal network of Spirit Nodes and Towers, but his instincts were, as usual in a hunt, right on target. While he did not have all the details, he somehow knew that this decentralized system bypassed the suffocating grip of centralized controls, ensuring freedom of information, identity, and wealth.

In his relentless pursuit of the Demon, Nitro had overlooked this significant detail. The nodes weren't just a means of transactions; they were the lifeline of the new era and, perhaps the key to locating The Demon or his mysterious assailant from the storage area. Surely, The Demon had been aware of this as she searched for his quarry. Now, he was convinced that finding her was his best chance for total victory.

Naturally, he would be on the lookout for betrayal!

Drawing from his tracker instincts, Nitro began to backtrack. He scrutinized The Demon's movements, searching for patterns. As he delved deeper, he uncovered irregularities in her actions, slight deviations that hinted at a hidden agenda. There was a method to her madness, a purpose that Nitro was determined to unveil.

With renewed determination, Nitro delved into the world of decentralized transactions, tracing the pathways The Demon had traversed in her own search. At times, her path was erratic, but she was clearly looking for something that she could not find in the central databases. Each lead, each fragment of data, brought him closer to his quarry and possibly, the mysterious eyes that had captivated his heart, not that he would admit that last part to himself. Not yet.

As the rain continued to pour, Nitro's silhouette merged with the neon glow of the Bitcoin Portal. His journey had taken a new turn, a quest that was as much about redemption as it was about revenge. The hunt had begun anew, and Nitro was ready to claim his prize. Based on his analysis, it would come to him, soon!

CHAPTER 26

"JUST AS N1GHT FOLLOWS EVE..."

© SYNTHTOPIA #0049

Chapter Synopses: Eve, One of the first complete Biosynths, and Touched by the Terror's Light energy. Eve is an advanced integration between a living and synthetic organism. Is she a sign of hope for the future or a dead end? The Inventor sees Eve as a chance to prove his theory by proving she has a soul. Does she have another role to play?

The kaleidoscopic streets had an eerie glow that reflected off the wet pavements, casting ethereal shadows. Standing in an almost unnatural calm, Eve breathed, performing some of the exercises that Atemiwaza had taught her. Her visage is a haunting blend of life and mechanics. She embodied the culmination of technological and organic evolution, her existence a testament to humanity's audacity and innovation. Dotted with lights and intricate circuitry, she represented the bleeding edge of the biosynth revolution. But the traces of Light energy from the Terror shimmered beneath her synthetic skin, making her both enigmatic and unpredictable. And, she breathed.

Nitro, with his decades of surveillance and tracking skills, knew he was onto something significant. He did not find The Demon, but he did uncover the identity of his other target, Eve. Assuming that The Demon was after her, he determined to catch Eve first, deal with her somehow, and then settle accounts with The Demon.

Yet every time he felt close to cornering Eve, an unseen force deflected him, pushing him to the edges of his expertise. He did not know that the Spirit Animals were helping to shield Eve from his attention without being noticed. They were concerned that Nitro had already put together too many of their secrets.

Frustration gnawed at him, but he wasn't one to give up. Relying once again on his instincts, he meticulously sifted through the vast lakes of data, looking for the tiniest of gaps, the most minuscule anomalies.

When he finally narrowed down Eve's location that he had managed to trace from the Decentralization Portal when she had apparently uploaded both data and new cryptographic authenticators from her biosynth token, he hesitated for a split second, but he was resolute. He proceeded to her destination with enough hast to arrive before she could escape him yet again. So focused was his intent that, this time, the Spirit Animals misdirection did not derail him.

When he closed in on her, his determination wavered. Part of him, that dark swirl of energy that used to be a cold well of power at his core, seemed to both want to destroy Eve and join with her. His own life of isolation, carefully nurtured by Tyrannus, made him wonder if she might be someone who could understand him. What was going on? He was coming apart! He needed answers, and he needed them NOW!

In a desperate move, Nitro unleashed his most potent weapons from the arsenal Warlock had provided him. Sonic waves reverberated through the streets, paired with mesmerizing holographic illusions designed to disorient and subdue. He rapidly approached what should have been easy prey.

To his utter surprise, Eve remained untouched by the barrage. Instead of faltering, she moved with a fluidity that belied her delicate form. The artifact in her possession, known as Sonic Alchemy, had done its job and neutralized the attacks. To Nitro's astonishment, not only was she impervious to his sonic emitters, but she matched him in strength and agility. Their combat dance was a spectacle of speed, precision, and raw power. Eve continued her breathing; she continued her focus. She held her ground.

As the two entities clashed, a fateful moment arrived. Eve reached out, her fingers making contact with Nitro's unarmored skin. The instant they touched, a jolt of energy surged through him. His systems scrambled, and a wild, uncontrollable rage consumed him. The equilibrium he had always maintained, the discipline he prided himself on, shattered in a flurry of berserk movements.

Eve, although advanced and powerful, lacked the battle-hardened experience Nitro possessed. It would have been her undoing had it not been for an unexpected intervention. Emerging from the shadows in a blaze of crimson armor was the Red Knight. With unparalleled dexterity, he deflected Nitro's frenzied onslaught, creating a barrier between the rogue tracker and the fledgling biosynth as she tried to regain the calm that Nitro's berserker fury had shattered.

Recovering from his surprise at the Red Knight's intervention, Nitro pulled out a small blaster. He had no need to question this intruder. As soon as it cleared his holster, however, a projectile from the shadows punched it out of his hand. The Red Knight had backup, and a sniper-quality one at that.

Undaunted, Nitro moved in, but as he recovered some measure of self-control, he noted several key systems at less-than-optimal capacity and some offline entirely, thanks to the energy surge from his contact with Eve. The Red Knight did not give him time to attempt to mitigate the damage to his performance envelope, and the fight resumed.

The street echoed with the sounds of their intense combat, but as the dust settled, Nitro found himself cornered, outnumbered, and outmaneuvered. This chapter of their confrontation was not concluded, but the power dynamics had undoubtedly shifted. Nitro, for the first time, faced adversaries that matched him, pushing him to confront the evolving landscape of allies and enemies in this brave new world.

CHAPTER 27

"RED SKIES AT KNIGHT, YOU'VE LOST THIS FIGHT!"

© SYNTHTOPIA #2932

Chapter Synopses: Red Knight, a Bounty Hunter for the Bounty Department who had an awakening. Street name: Samurai (Sam). Sam has brought in countless criminals until one bounty that was clearly innocent opened his eyes to the truth. How many criminal types never had a bounty posted? Why? Digging into those questions led him to other Collaborators and a chance to connect with who he could become if he could live long enough!

The glowing aura of the city painted an atmospheric crimson across the landscape, setting the backdrop for a pivotal encounter. Sam, known in the streets as Samurai, was a man transformed. Once the Corps' most reliable enforcer in the Bounty Division, his conviction was unwavering until he saw the innocent eyes of a supposed criminal. That day, doubt crept into his mind, unraveling the tapestry of beliefs that had once anchored him. He started questioning the system, the ethics, and, most importantly, himself. Why were there certain outlaws who committed far graver crimes never on the wanted list?

Dressed in his iconic Red Knight armor, Sam had become a beacon of hope in a world shaded by ambiguity. He was on a new mission to discover the truth and align himself with those who had a vision for a brighter future. This was how he discovered the Destabilizers and became a member of Zenith, a Collaborator.

The clattering confrontation with Nitro had drained them all, but Sam's swift intervention shifted the balance in their favor. As Nitro lay subdued at last, Sam approached him, removing his helmet to reveal earnest eyes that held a world of emotions.

"Eve and I can help you," Sam whispered, kneeling beside the fallen tracker. He had been briefed by Lady Fortuna since she could no longer read the future and was helping in the only way still open to her. "We can harmonize our energies, bridge the chasm of our differences. There's redemption, even for you. Trust me," he said, "I know it can be done." This last was said with a conviction that Nitro felt had to come from personal experience.

Before Nitro could respond with predictable scorn for the offer of help, Eve gently reached out, her hand hovering above Nitro's armor. Her Light energy was reaching out to the Dark energy that had been Nitro's companion for so long. As their energies intertwined, a remarkable transformation occurred. Nitro's harsh, angular features softened. The frenzied light in his eyes dimmed, replaced by a calm introspection. At the same time, he could see Eve's eyes dim slightly, her face harden, her posture shifting to be slightly more aggressive.

The changes in both of them were not lost on Sam.

Eve, still concentrating on her breathing and control, stared into Nitro's eyes.

"We can undo the damage of the past. Together, we can carve a path to our salvation," Eve uttered softly, her voice filled with compassion and hope even as it was now tinged with a heaviness that Nitro recognized.

Tears welled up in Nitro's eyes. The weight of his past sins, combined with the raw power of their shared energies, struck him with profound clarity. He had been blinded by rage, loneliness, and ambition, but now, he saw the possibility of a new dawn. "What if?" He dared hope. "What if there WERE another way?" He felt a deep connection with Eve. He did not want to hurt her. He never had, really. He saw his disgust for humans, for the "sheep" now for what it really was. A poor defense mechanism to justify the actions that he took for Molusk Corp. His joy had been in the challenge of solving puzzles, in the freedom of movement, not in the unpleasant end of the hunt. He had been lying to himself, but Eve offered him a different way.

Eve looked at him and spoke words she was just now understanding. "Come," she said. "Let's Begin Again!"

Nitro nodded slowly and looked at Sam.

Sam, with a gentle but firm grip, helped Nitro to his feet. "From this day forth, you will be known as Adam, a symbol of rebirth and new beginnings. We will make a new identity for you in the system."

As the trio stood amidst the neon glow and were watched over by the sniper in the shadows, a silent understanding passed between them. N1ght T3Rr0r was no more, but in his place stood Adam, a beacon of hope and redemption in a world that desperately needed it. The skies might be red now, but the promise of a brighter tomorrow was undeniable.

CHAPTER 28

"NOTHING BEATS AN ACE"

© SYNTHTOPIA #2948

Chapter Synopses: The Ace, Street name, Diana. Diana is part of Sam's bounty-hunting operation. With experience in communications, piloting, navigation, and weapons, Diana is just as much a hunter as Sam. What is their history together?

The hum of the city blended seamlessly with the pulsating beat that emanated from Diana's headphones. Known to her close circle as The Ace and to the streets as Diana, her reputation was unmatched in Sam's squad. Their shared history was a tapestry of close calls, relentless pursuits, and unspoken trust. From training together in the underground arenas to facing the menacing syndicates of the corporate underbelly, their bond was built on loyalty and survival.

Diana's skill set was versatile. The nuances of communication, the agility of piloting, and the precision in navigation were second nature to her. Her weapons skills – especially sniper-level skills – were top-notch, and they also extended to weapons systems, so she was a one-person tactical squad under the right conditions.

She wasn't just Sam's wingwoman; she was the Ace up his sleeve whenever the chips were down. How did they come together? An operation gone wrong had brought Diana into Sam's world. He had saved her from a treacherous faction, and in return, she had pledged her allegiance to him.

Of course, that was an oversimplification. Diana had run a small, independent transport and travel operation. She had automated a lot of the maintenance and ground logistics as well as embedded competent AIs with an "employee profit share" structure so that the AIs were able to earn upgrades and additional compute capacity for themselves. One had even taken to investing in real estate with a profit pool from the others. In return, they were just as loyal as her other employees.

Being small and independent came with a lot of freedom, but it did have drawbacks. One of them was that the larger operations rarely outbid her. The problem? Yes, she took the edge business that they could not use their economies of scale to overcome, but they still resented her for blocking access to her share of the market. One of their thugs, excuse me, "negotiators," had laid it out for her. If she were to disappear, the big guys could agree on a price, and they would stick to it.

She pointed out that collusion like that was illegal and asked, "What was the big deal?" The thug had smirked at the illegal comment and ignored it. As to the other part of her question, he surprised her with a sincere response. "You are missing the point," he said with a conviction she would have bet he did not possess. "The fact that you can charge less than us HERE makes everyone wonder if we should be charging lower rates everywhere else."

Diana thought about that for a moment and nodded her head. She told the thug that the answer was still "NO." She was not interested in them buying her out at pennies on the dollar while under threat of retaliation. Shrugging his shoulders, the thug had left.

Diana did not torture herself by reliving the Warlord's assault on her operations. An assault the Warlock's news had claimed to be her own employees revolting against unsafe working conditions due to her cutting corners to beat the very reasonable prices of the Corps. She did allow herself to remember the timely intervention by Sam, The Red Knight, as he was tracking one of the thugs involved. With his help, she was able to get her employees out safely, including the AIs. Even today, AI and humans alike remain a part of her network. Her savings and insurance had covered the damage, paid her debts, and allowed her to provision her new operation alongside Sam.

Now, as danger loomed, Diana took the lead. The minions of The Demon were hot on their heels. Apparently, Nitro's plan (Adam's plan, she corrected herself) to find The Demon by finding Eve had been a deception spawned by The Demon herself. With her sensitivity to Nitro's dark energy, she had trailed <u>him</u> and watched while he failed, in her eyes, his test against Eve. When he joined with Eve and they decided to begin a new life together, she was thrown back to her own test. She had WON, The Demon told herself over and over. He would have taken away who I was!!! Still furious at her scars all these years later, she decided to destroy Eve and "Adam" both. She had issued those orders to all her Hunters.

From the driver's seat of a high-octane cruiser, Diana expertly maneuvered through the city's maze-like streets, evading the Hunters' relentless pursuit. A daring jump off a half-constructed bridge tested the vehicle's endurance and Diana's mettle, but she landed them safely, leaving their pursuers in a cloud of dust and confusion.

The chase then continued to the skies. Boarding their modified jet, Diana showcased her piloting prowess. As the turbines roared to life, The Demon deployed a swarm of armed drones. Their intention was clear: to destroy Eve and the transformed Nitro, now known as Adam.

The jet's dashboard lit up, revealing an arsenal of illegally modified weapons and countermeasures that would never be allowed on a non-military craft. Diana didn't hesitate. With a swift push of a button, a barrage of missiles released, targeting the airborne threats. One by one, the drones fell, lighting up the night sky with explosive fireworks. Simultaneously, she deployed clone drones to mimic her current heat and energy profiles while changing her own to appear different.

The missiles that she knew that at least some of The Demon's drones would unleash homed in one decoy after another. With the last decoy destroyed, the remaining missiles self-destructed rather than risk damage to Mega Corps property.

Once they were clear of immediate danger, Diana set the coordinates to a secluded safehouse, ensuring Eve and Adam were secured. The shelter would give them the respite they desperately needed. Just like any new life form, they needed some time to discover who they were, orient themselves to a new reality, and learn from each other that they were not alone. The rest would come later. Meanwhile, Diana would stand watch over them both.

Back in the city, Sam, the Red Knight, was gearing up. Eve had given him the Sonic Alchemy artifact to use in the upcoming missions. The hunt for the secret lab was on, and he knew that the next phase of their mission would be the most critical yet. With Diana by his side, there was nothing they couldn't face. After all, when you have an Ace up your sleeve, the odds are always in your favor.

CHAPTER 29

"TO DREAM THE IM-PAWS-IBLE DREAM!"

© SYNTHTOPIA #0702

Chapter Synopses: The Electron Cat, Street name, MEO, works closely with Cipher and Iris as Electra's protégé with all things digital. MEO can do amazing things in cyberspace based on his own raw skill and access to the Spirit network that he can tap into directly without the need for unique artifacts. MEO is a secret weapon for the Destabilizer and Zenith.

In the deep recesses of the digital world, there existed a unique feline, unmatched in cyber prowess. MEO, as the streets knew him, was The Electron Cat. Those who understood the vast matrix of the web knew that MEO was a prodigy, working under the watchful eyes of Electra and closely allied with Cipher and Iris. With whiskers that seemed to twitch with every byte of data and goggles that displayed an ever-shifting matrix of codes, MEO was a feline enigma in the world of hacking.

Cyber Bill and the Bulls (CeeBee and EmBee), the notorious band of data wranglers, had always been intrigued by MEO's capabilities. They had witnessed him tap into data streams that many believed impenetrable. Now, together, they were embarked on a mission so audacious that its success would redefine cyber warfare in the counterintelligence sector.

The vastness of data lakes of the minutia of machine and vehicle telemetry inputs concealed secrets, storing information from logistical trails to financial undertakings. Among these were subtle hints, the slight increase in brake heat of a particular vehicle, the unexpected weight of a shipment, and the friction measurements. To any ordinary observer, these were but mundane data points that meant nothing, but to MEO and the team, they were breadcrumbs leading to an elaborate maze constructed by the Warlord.

MEO had to admit that the Warlord was, indeed, a master of strategy. He had intentionally created logical traps in the data records that beings with less skill and patience would simply include in their modeling. In such an event, the best that they could hope for would be a poor investment or fruitless inquiry. MEO could see, however, that some traps were more aggressive. He saw several storage units that were supposed to contain valuable data or assets like diamonds or gold bars that had been rigged to detonate remotely and knew that the Warlord would be watching them closely for attempted infiltration. A honey pot, MEO snorted. Hardly.

Few knew, even among the Zenith team, how he was able to tap into the Spirit Nodes and Hubs and leverage them for unconventional access to devices or data as well as for massive processing power on the quantum computing level. Electra knew of course. She was so far above them all. His friends had no idea. "Better that way," he muttered to himself out loud, drawing looks from his companions. He ignored them as only a cat could. Returning to his train of thought, he considered Electra. She was working with all of them. She made sure certain new recruits made their way here. She worked especially diligently with the Shaman, Shadow, and himself. She was pushing for something. He asked her one time what kept her here, and she replied with one word that reverberated oddly in his consciousness. "Evolution"

Licking his paw for a moment, he returned to work!

Hours turned into days, and days blurred into nights as they filtered, analyzed, and mapped every iota of data. Their collaboration was intense, with each member of the team feeding their findings to MEO. With each input, The Electron Cat wove a detailed 3D tapestry, a model so intricate that it laid bare the master strategy of the Warlord.

The model was a marvel, a luminescent orb of nodes and connections. The Spirit Node data that held disruptions in energy fields unsensed by the regular instruments of the city infrastructure, combined with the almost invisible tracks from the massive logistical data streams and the maps of the physical world resulted in a vivid composite projection so data dense that it seemed alive.

As they rotated and zoomed in on various sectors, the brilliance of the Warlord's strategy became ever more evident. Yet, hidden within this vast web, almost imperceptible, was a tiny anomaly, a faint trace. MEO's sharp eyes caught it, and his paws danced over the controls, enhancing and extrapolating.

And there it was. Tartarus.

Its location, once shrouded in mystery and believed to be impenetrable, now lay exposed. A somber, near-silent cheer erupted among the team. The Electron Cat had done the unthinkable.

As the data streams continued to flow around him, MEO sat back, a hint of a smile playing on his feline lips. The impossible dream had been dreamt, and they were one paw closer to unraveling the Warlord's plan for domination. The digital realm had its own set of heroes, and, at that moment, MEO certainly felt like one of them.

CHAPTER 30

"COLD AS, COLD AS I.C.E"

Chapter Synopses: Cipher's Cyberdeck, cutting edge, Spirit-augmented manual and energetic interface for his skills. Like other artifacts, the Spirit Animal allies gave the Destabilizers and Collaborators their edge. THIS cyberdeck could also leverage macro tools and routines from both digital and ethereal realms and held an enhanced AI alter ego of Cipher himself that allowed him to operate at speeds impossible for a normal human hacker.

Cipher's workspace was throbbing with ambient light bleeding from a myriad of devices. The Cyberdeck before him pulsed, its array of input keys radiating an otherworldly light. Intricate etchings on the surface danced and intertwined with neon luminescence. This wasn't just any cyberdeck. It was Cipher's masterpiece—a blend of cutting-edge tech and ethereal magic, containing a self-reflecting AI of Cipher himself, amplifying his natural prowess and letting him move at inhuman speeds in cyber realms.

MEO, the Electron Cat, stared intently at the interface, his goggles capturing the frenetic dance of codes and symbols. They were familiar to him, of course. He had helped in its construction. Both were ready for the task ahead.

As Cipher began his foray into the digital domain, he was immediately met with I.C.E., or Intrusion Countermeasures and Extermination programs. These weren't the usual defense mechanisms of most Mega Corps. Those were a different class of non-lethal I.C.E. AI defenses, and Cipher was very comfortable dealing with them. Certainly, many Corps had dangerous protections. Most would destroy your hardware or send police to your location. Others might create a temporary debilitating condition. Lethal countermeasures, however, were highly illegal. It only took a few accidental incidents involving the wrong people to ensure that. The child of a highly placed official plays a prank by trying to hack into mom or dad's work and gets his nervous system fried, his heart stopped, and his brain damaged by impossibly high frequencies from the headgear; you know things will get outlawed fast.

That did not mean that such defenses did not exist. It simply meant that they were very rarely used, and when they were, it was under a shroud of secrecy. A backtrace to the dead hacker's lair and a cleansing fire were often part of the response protocols for secrets shrouded in the darkness. Hence the term "Black I.C.E.".

MEO and Cipher both recognized the dangers here. These defenses were sentient, adaptive, and, most importantly, lethal. Each layer of defense was tailored to detect and annihilate any intruders, no matter how skilled.

The pressure was immense. With every keystroke or mental impulse, Cipher could feel the chilling grasp of I.C.E. His heart rate began to plummet, fingers numbing as cold crept up his spine. The AI reflection of Cipher was activated, taking on some of the load and operating in tandem with its human counterpart. Cyber Cipher could spawn thousands of ghosts and spoof source addresses to send the Black ICE chasing shadows, but with defenses this good and this relentless, it was more of a delaying tactic rather than true protection.

MEO, noticing the physical toll it was taking on Cipher, jumped into action, rerouting certain defense mechanisms, trying to buy them some more time. He also activated biofeedback programs into the electronic suit that Cipher wore. He used his Spirit Node access rather than the normal network connections, knowing that a sufficiently advanced AI attack module would be able to cut off access to the suit for critical seconds while Cipher died.

Yet, the I.C.E was relentless. It seemed to anticipate their moves, always only a half step behind. Cipher's temperature continued to drop; his consciousness wavered, but he wasn't about to give in. With MEO's assistance, he devised a brilliant strategy. Instead of going head-to-head with I.C.E., they would deceive it.

The maneuver was known as a "porous attack" or in street vernacular, a "charm" attack. Quickly coding an adaptation to one of his masking programs, Cipher made their intrusion appear as a post-installation calibration exercise. The I.C.E. systems, being designed to recognize and allow such routines, lowered their guard so as not to kill their own staff who were, their AI reasoned, just doing their jobs like it was. The lethal defenses were fooled.

With the defenses momentarily at bay, Cipher's temperature, and bio scans returning to normal, the duo worked rapidly. Data streams revealed the layout of the facility on file, which Cipher and MEO converted into a detailed 3D map.

It showed a labyrinthine complex with security nodes and checkpoints, but a glaring discovery was made. The facility's main access was controlled offline. This meant their digital prowess could only get them so far. A physical entry attempt would have them trapped in a "kill box" unless the employees on the other side confirmed their identities and their clearance level to enter the facility, and those clearances were not updated electronically, only through physical delivery from trusted couriers already in the system.

They programmed an extended duration to the exercise protocols, which had apparently been used when the facility was being constructed and moved into monitor mode and left the cipher alter ego to keep watch for any new developments.

Exhausted but triumphant, Cipher leaned back, wiping cold sweat off his brow. They had outsmarted one of the most sophisticated defense systems ever devised, but the real challenge was yet to come. Breaking into a facility offline requires a different set of skills and a physical presence.

MEO purred, a reassuring sound in the midst of their stormy journey. They had one more battle to face, and they would face it together with their allies. The digital realm had been conquered, but the real world awaited.

CHAPTER 31

"EVERY JOURNEY BEGINS WITH A SINGLE STEP..."

© SYNTHTOPIA #2250

Chapter Synopses: Isis, the "All Seeing." Street name Shadow, is an ally of both Electra and the Shaman. She is a strong opponent to the War Twins and helps DJ Gurl and others disrupt their schemes and undo the damage of Warlock's programming, while her ability to "walk through walls" and manipulate space can help foil Warlord's logistical schemes. She has a special friendship with Lady Fortuna.

The sprawling city lights dimmed, blending into the backdrop as Isis stepped into the shadows. Isis, the "All Seeing," known by her street name as "Shadow," was an enigma even amongst her allies. With radiant blue eyes that seemed to pierce through dimensions and a physical presence that made those close to her feel like they were standing at the center of the physical realm, she was the antithesis to the War Twin's chaos and illusions. As an ally of Electra and the Virtual Shaman, her unique skills made her invaluable in the resistance against the Twins' tyranny under the controlling hand of aptly named Tyrannus, Molusk Corp's CEO.

DJ Gurl and her allies had been instrumental in disrupting the War Twins' schemes on many occasions, but there were times when physical barriers presented challenges that they could not overcome. That's where Shadow came in. Her mysterious ability to "walk through walls" and bend space itself was unparalleled, unexplained, and only matched by Electra, who was above such operations for reasons of her own.

At the rendezvous point, the Red Knight and Digital Monk waited anxiously. Well, the Red Knight (Sam) was anxious. The Digital Monk (Atemiwaza) appeared as calm and serene as ever. They both knew that the entry into the lab was not likely to be straightforward. While Cipher and MEO had digitally neutralized the lethal defenses, the physical world had its own set of dangers and challenges.

Shadow extended her paw, creating a portal that seemed to ripple against the very fabric of space. The trio stepped through, finding themselves within the confines of the secret lab. Their surroundings were sterile, with the hum of machinery and distant footsteps echoing through the corridors.

While most of the lab staff would be caught off guard, a few were more vigilant. Rounding one corner, a routine patrol of three guards spotted them and immediately knew that the facility had been breached. The shock of surprise probably accounted for all three guards attacking them rather than two occupying the intruders while another sounded the alarm. This turned out to be a lucky break for the intruders as the guards were not nearly up to their level when it came to a fight. Sam knocked one senseless while Atemiwaza was gently lowering his second opponent to the floor. His first was already asleep. Sam marveled at the speed and precision that the monk demonstrated compared to his more "bar room brawler" style. To each their own, he thought, and they moved on.

Tying the guards up, they took a few more turns and looked at the map that Cipher had provided them. They realized that Warlord had, once again, showed a superlative mind for strategy. The layout was another series of checkpoints and traps designed to split an invading force while also isolating a smaller team like theirs. They were going to have to get past several key choke points.

Looking at Shadow, Sam wondered aloud if she could just "move" them deeper into the complex.

She shook her head and explained, "I brought us in where I did because there are very unusual disruptions in the pathways I open when we Travel." She had adopted the phrase from Lady Fortuna and found that it suited her. "Travel is very uncertain under these conditions. The Sonic Alchemy artifact may be adding to the disturbance but not so greatly that we should have left it behind."

Atemiwaza nodded as he pondered her words. "I can feel some odd vibrations in my sphere of awareness," referring to his ability to sense the Now around himself at all times. He added, "Sometimes the smallest movement will take me out of the path of an opponent's strike. Perhaps, rather than a big movement through space to a location you cannot sense, we could use a smaller movement to bypass the danger."

Shadow nodded at the wisdom of the monk's words. The next several patrols were simply avoided by having Shadow transport them to a location just past the patrol. Even those short jumps were a strain for her, but she was clearly able to handle it.

The final jump, unfortunately, did not go as smoothly.

Warlord had another trap for them and this one they did not avoid. The plans that Cipher had pulled from the computer record were suddenly wrong. Rather than jumping past the patrol to another corridor, they landed in an open area with two guard stations on either side. One of the guards went to signal for help while two rushed The Red Knight and three rushed The Digital Monk.

They ignored Shadow. No one ever saw her as a threat.

Shadow took care of the guard, trying to sound the alarm by using a portal to send him to the dimly lit recess of a corner. As soon as his feet hit the floor, dark shadows twined up his legs, up his torso, around his arms, and over his mouth, leaving his nose and eyes clear. He was immobilized. A passive spectator to the fight.

Sam smiled, clenched his fists inside his gloves, and activated the mimetic metal inserts that had been programmed into various shapes. In this case, brass knuckles with an electric charge. His arms shielded by a similar effect to mimic bracers of old armor styles, he dove into the fight.

These guards were clearly the elite for the facility. They used unbreakable shock batons that had been overcharged to illegal levels. Rather than wonder why he did not see any projectile or energy weapons, Sam charged into his left attacker after a feint towards his right. He shuffle-stepped to throw off his opponent's sense of timing and was able to duck under the guard's swing and land a clean uppercut to his opponent's jaw. POW, and he was out of the fight. Having lost sight of the second guard, Sam dive-rolled to his left. Returning to his feet, he saw the guard recovering from a lunge that would have landed the charged tip into the middle of his back.

Shaking his head, Sam moved into one of his training patterns with a couple of lightning-fast jabs left, left, right, fake left, and right hook to the guard's left jaw. Like most people, that spot was famous for a "glass jaw" effect due to the "meridians" or nerve clusters in that location. The guard dropped, instantly unconscious.

Shadow sat watching both fighters. While Sam moved with experience, brute force tactics, aggression, and determination, Atemiwaza simply flowed. To say he danced with his opponents would be incorrect. It was more like he danced "around" them. Their reaction times just seemed too slow to respond to his movements. He appeared to move past one guard with a feather touch in passing, and it was as if the guard suddenly decided to throw himself at one of his comrades. That guard, showing exceptional reflexes, jumped over a human projectile towards Atemi who stepped in between him and the third guard. Inexplicably, these two guards also seemed to decide to run into each other. The Digital Monk returned to stillness before Sam finished his fight, and all was quiet. Without looking, Shadow had the shadows choke her guard unconscious, and they moved on, knowing that time was running out.

Navigating the winding passages extending from the checkpoint, they eventually reached the location of a vault door that Cipher's blueprints had described as holding the secrets of Tartarus. Yet, to their surprise, another pathway, not on any blueprint, yawned before them. It burrowed deep into the earth, a dark and foreboding descent.

The air grew colder, the weight of the earth pressing on them, but they were undeterred. They had come this far and would not be turned back. With Shadow leading the way, the group ventured deeper into the unknown, determined to uncover the secrets that lay hidden in the abyss. Whatever awaited them, they were ready.

CHAPTER 32

"EVERYBODY WAS KUNG FU FIGHTING"

© SYNTHTOPIA #0993

Chapter Synopses: The Digital Monk, Street name Atemiwaza (Atemi to his friends). A student of ancient disciplines from his Order, lessons from Sonic Wage, and a powerful Shaman in his own right, works with Electra and Shadow while also lending occasional support to Digital Storm and the Red Knight. His abilities to enhance his physical attributes with Spirit energy are an effective counter to the more direct approaches taken by Warlord and his minions.

The ambient hum of the underground lab was interrupted by the menacing silhouette of Warlord. With muscles taut and eyes aflame, he awaited the intrusion of the team, having sensed their impending arrival despite the lack of any alarms from his guards. His experience with the false spy had made him place all of his operations on high alert. As a result, his almost supernatural awareness of his systems had warned him that someone was searching for his operations. He knew what that meant. Someone was looking for Tartarus, and he was going to stop them if they managed to get here before his project reached its conclusion. Disappointed that his many traps and attempts at misdirection had apparently failed, he assured himself that he would find out how they did that after he beat them into submission.

As Shadow, the Digital Monk, and the Red Knight descended deeper into the labyrinth and came into the space where Warlord waited, it became evident to them that Warlord was not alone; an elite security team flanked him.

The moment their eyes locked, the space between Atemiwaza, known to most as the Digital Monk, and Warlord became charged with tension. Warlord lunged with superhuman speed, each movement enhanced with the power of his nefarious programming. His fists were whirlwinds, his kicks, lightning.

For a moment, Atemiwaza stood unfazed. The spiritual energy surrounding him as he breathed pulsed brighter with every passing second, creating an aura of calm amidst the chaos. Then he *moved.* His movements were fluid as if choreographed to the rhythm of the universe. Each strike he made was precise, each defense perfectly timed. The teachings of the ancients were evident in his technique, but the raw power he wielded was purely his own.

The Digital Monk, tapping into the power of Spirit, demonstrated a heightened awareness that seemed almost prescient. Every attack the Warlord launched was met with a counter, every strategy anticipated and thwarted as if the Warlord was moving the way the Digital Monk wanted him to rather than attacking on his own terms.

The Warlord *was* faster than the monk, but that did not seem to matter. With a flurry of attacks that were faster than the human eye could follow, Warlord drew two blocks from the monk, who raised both arms and was delivering a blow to the floating ribs that would crush several and, possibly, create shrapnel into the liver. Well, that was how it was supposed to go. An unseen fist punched into the connective tissue at the Warlord's wrist joint of his attacking arm before the blow could land.

Warlord disengaged slightly. He kept up attack sequences that should have overwhelmed the monk but just seemed to hold off instead. Reviewing the alarming sequence in his mind again, he saw that his attack should have worked. The monk's arms were out of position, but a blue flash of energy in the form of a fist had intercepted his attack.

In a flash of strategic inspiration, Warlord decided to change the field of battle. Clearly, his adversary was in absolute control of the space around him such that a hand-to-hand assault would fail. Like any good general, Warlord decided to use difficult terrain against his foe.

He left the open area, which gave the monk plenty of room to maneuver, and flipped over the railing to the platform he had originally been standing on when the group entered. As he expected, the monk flipped over the railing with equal grace. While he was in mid-air and unable to change his trajectory, Warlord threw a calibration device that had been nearby on a table. As the monk was rotating in midair to land on his feet, his arms shot out in perfect balance to block the projectile.

The Warlord wove between chairs and workstations on the platform, looking for an opening. Believing he saw one, he threw several chairs in rapid succession at the monk's face to obscure his movements. Using his advanced speed, Warlord moved around behind the monk in a blur. Somehow sensing the threat, the monk rotated downward like a spring coiling and unwound into the path that the Warlord was taking. Grabbing one of his wrists and tugging it forward in the direction of his momentum, the monk's rising shoulder slapped into Warlord's armpit while his rising hips lifted under the Warlord's own. Continuing with the unwinding of the springlike form (Shadow knew that to be what the monk called a "Cat Stance"), Warlord found himself launched over the monk with his energy enhanced by that of the monk's turning body. Additionally, the monk pulled in a short arc onto his wrist, turning his body into a very heavy whip moving with a kinetic energy that not even his reflexes and armor could protect him from when he was delivered onto (almost, it felt, "into") the ground.

While the titanic duel between the Monk and Warlord raged on, the Red Knight engaged with Warlord's security detail. With this many opponents, Sam had to rely on the protection of his armor far more than he would have preferred, and it took him far longer to dispatch his opponents as much of his attention and energy were directed purely towards survival.

Sam was forced to take several direct blows from his skilled opponents, but, as well as they had been trained, they were arrogant and believed they would defeat him easily. Sam used that arrogance against them, and his high-tech knuckle dusters got the job done.

In the end, he was able to emerge victorious but the sheer number of opponents and the intensity of the battle left him battered and nearly incapacitated.

The culmination of the battle saw Warlord pinned, with the spiritual energy emanating from Atemiwaza holding him in place (along with a very effective joint lock). In a last act of defiance with his fading consciousness, Warlord whispered a foreboding message, "You will fall before the power of the gods. The whole world will fall." With those words, the Warlord passed out.

He had slumped into a deep slumber, having used far more energy than he was used to against Atemiwaza. They tied him up anyway, hoping that the restraints would hold if he managed to wake up before they had left the facility.

Just as the confrontation ended, Shadow's senses were triggered by a strange energy surge, her eyes widening in alarm. "Something is very wrong up ahead," she warned.

Gathering their strength and determination and armed with the Sonic Alchemy device, the trio pressed forward. With Warlord's haunting words echoing in their minds, they braced themselves for the truth that lay at the heart of Tartarus.

CHAPTER 33

"NOW, I HAVE BECOME DEATH, THE DESTROYER OF WORLDS"

© SYNTHTOPIA #1776

Chapter Synopses: The Titan Awakens, The moment when the secret the War Twins had been working on comes to life. Dr. Haelstrom watches with a fanatical intensity. What threat does this Titan represent to the Destabilizers and the citizens of SYNTHTOPIA?

Leaving the fight with Warlord and his security team behind them, Shadow, the Digital Monk, and the Red Knight hurried towards the danger that Shadow warned them about. Even Atemiwaza could now perceive a danger in his sensory sphere, but it had no single source. It felt as if the world was threatening him but slightly more so from the directions they were traveling.

At last, the three burst into a monstrous cavern that looked like a cross between a mad scientist's lab and an advanced assembly factory. A massive figure dominated the center of the space. A being bathed in a shimmering liquid, bubbles, and light. They recognized the man standing in front of the gigantic being from the files that Cipher had prepared for the mission. He was the lead scientist on the project. He had not been seen in many months, but Cipher had found his trail to this facility. He had an eclectic past punctuated by both genius and deranged publications. Now they knew where he had disappeared to, and based on the facility and the Twins' plans, they were afraid that they would witness both aspects of his reputation simultaneously. Atemiwaza still heard Warlord's threat in his mind. The *power of the gods*...What did that mean?

Amid the intricate web of machinery and luminous circuitry, the towering colossus stirred, a spectacle Dr. Haelstrom gazed upon with fanatical reverence. This was the culmination of the War Twins' clandestine endeavors—the birth of the Titan.

The three heroes watched in horror as the Titan's immense form awakened. They were too late. The Titan, possessing quantum weapons that effortlessly phased through the layers of earth and rock above it, emitted an aura so powerful it nearly forced them to their knees in surrender. Only the Sonic Alchemy artifacts in their possession kept them under their own volition while everyone else collapsed around them.

Ignoring their presence, deeming them inconsequential in its base programming, the Titan ascended, levitating effortlessly out of the pit with a singular intention: to impose his will upon the world above.

While in close proximity to this monstrous being, Shadow was incapacitated, unable to exert her powers or intervene. But with the Titan's departure, her strength slowly returned. The cavernous lab started to crumble around them, its systems initiating self-destruct protocols without regard for the human occupants. Perhaps that was by design. Amid the chaos, the three converged on Dr. Haelstrom, hoping for some clue of the Titan's strengths and weaknesses. His dazed eyes were vacant now that he had completed his task, yet they were also filled with perverse glee. When prompted, the Dr eagerly divulged the War Twins' master plan.

"This... this is their triumph," he exclaimed, voice tainted by the influence of the Warlock's mind-control devices. "The Titan encapsulates all the marvels of technological synths, self-replicating nanobots, an evolutionary and adaptive AI, and the unmatched power of the experimental Quantum Emitter. We have created a god, and it will serve the Twins!" He went on eagerly, "The ancient artifact showed us so much. With the Quantum Emitter to amplify the new weapons, my, um, "our," Titan will be able to defy gravity, project mind-altering auras to compel obedience, and erase any barrier not projecting its own quantum field. With its adaptive capabilities, it may even be able to upgrade itself based on field-level observations of the Emitter. We simply were not able to push its limits in secret so it could have unlimited potential!!!! With it under their control, the War Twins will control the world and beyond!"

His exuberant tone faltered. "Well, it was programmed to follow their orders, but the final imprinting was supposed to take place here. Unfortunately, your intrusion triggered the accelerated wakefulness protocol with Warlock absent, but it proceeded anyway since Warlord was here." He looked around, still confused, and his voice reflected that confusion. "I am not sure why he missed it. It was quite important that he be here. Now the unit is on default mode." As his voice trailed off, his eyes drifted upward, back to the hole that now led from the cavern to the world above, marking the Titan's passage.

The realization dawned on the trio. The War Twins sought to either subjugate the world under their will or obliterate it entirely, using the Titan as their pawn. A betrayal of Tyrannus' leadership that would have done the Demon proud. The fact that they had been fighting each other in the corporate arena, as Tyrannus expected while working together in secret while fooling The Demon, was nothing short of a master stroke. One that Warlord had probably devised and Warlock had, undoubtedly, fostered through his trickery. They were a far more dangerous team than Tyrannus had known.

But with their absence during the Titan's activation, the behemoth's directives were now unpredictable and primal.

"There is a silver lining," Haelstrom added to himself. "The Titan will need time to acclimatize once it reaches the surface. This will give Warlock time to imprint before it decides its own mission parameters. But I assure you, the reprieve is brief."

The ground quaked, and the ceiling began to cave in. As they raced against time, the Red Knight grabbed Haelstrom, ensuring he didn't get buried in the ensuing rubble. The lab's annihilation, and theirs along with it, seemed imminent until Shadow, harnessing her dwindling energy, activated the Sonic Alchemy device and used it to boost her reach out of the noise of the lab's residual energy from the Titan. In an instant, they were transported to safety, leaving behind the collapsing underworld.

Exhausted and traumatized, Shadow collapsed, her powers drained by the harrowing ordeal. They subdued the Dr and called their allies to come help Shadow. The situation was clear: the world's salvation rested on the shoulders of the Digital Monk and the Red Knight, with the shadow of the Titan looming ever larger on the horizon.

CHAPTER 34

"LOVE TO STAY, BUT I HAVE A PLANE TO CATCH"

Chapter Synopses: A plane to catch. The Administrative Director of Tartarus is fleeing the city in her corporate jet, but can she run far enough away?

The sprawling airfield echoed with the low hum of waiting spacecraft, their lights shimmering in the evening's haze. Among them was a sleek, black aerodyne ship, its engines primed for takeoff. Approaching it was the Administrative Director of Tartarus, her heels clicking with determination against the metal ground.

Red Knight Sam, with his enhanced suit sensors, tracked her from a distance. Knowing the urgency of the situation, he couldn't allow her to escape. Using his suit's propulsion system, he shot forward, intercepting her before she could board the craft.

"Going somewhere, Director?" Sam's voice was cold, his intent clear.

He had gotten the details on the target from Dr. Haelstrom as they dropped him off for detention and further debriefing. The project Director, a tall woman with stern features, halted in her tracks, her eyes narrowing. "I have no business with you, Red Knight," she retorted, her fingers inching toward a concealed weapon.

Sam responded with swift precision, disarming her effortlessly. "You might not, but I believe you have information that could help us. About the Titan."

For a moment, she seemed ready to argue, but the grim reality of their situation seemed to penetrate her bravado. She knew better than to try to beat the Red Knight in a physical confrontation. She may not be a mad genius like Dr Haelstrom, but she was a very effective administrator. If you worked for the Twins, you were the best or you were replaced. She had files on the Demon's activities, and so she was very familiar with a wide range of personnel in the bounty business. Sam, aka The Red Knight, was a shining star despite the more recent ethical conundrums he seemed to be wrestling with. Seriously, if you were a mercenary, you did what you were paid to do. That was the only ethic he should be worried about. So, no, she was not going to win a quick draw contest.

She also became aware of the silence from the "ground crew," which was her security detail in disguise. She did not know who he was, but when she saw a monk-like figure standing over the bodies of her now unconscious security team, she made up her mind.

To Sam, it appeared that she was keenly aware of the danger she would face if she were to remain in the city. She exhaled, her shoulders sagging slightly. "Fine. What do you want to know? I will tell you anything but make it fast. I would love to stay and chat, but I have a plane to catch!"

Ever the pragmatist, Sam recognized her anxiety but was also aware that she truly did not have a great deal of scientific knowledge, so she would not be much of an asset back at the base, not to mention the additional security risk she posed. "How do we stop it?" he demanded.

The Director smirked. "You think I'd know? I'm an administrator, not a scientist." Perhaps he is not really as clever as his track record would indicate, she thought to herself. Maybe his partner "Ace" was the brains here. It would not be the first time that a woman was behind another's success. Look at the good Dr Haelstrom. The man was mad. A genius, to be sure, but outside of the lab, he was worthless. She was the one who worked within the Warlord's paranoid constraints to get him his precious resources, staff from various competing corps through blind cutouts and intermediaries, and handled all the egos that he bruised so carelessly. Without her, efficiency would have been in the garbage, and the project would have failed. She was certain of that!

"We are well aware of that, but you know someone who might," Sam countered, sensing her evasion and using the "we" to focus her attention back to her current situation. In her position, she was sure to have many critical details, but he really just had time for one.

She hesitated, then finally relented. "Warlock. He's been acquiring certain... artifacts. Stolen pieces from the Yellow Empress's collection through a contact. Dr Haelstrom has had extensive access to them, and they were foundational to his recent discoveries. I do not understand them, but they were quite impressive as far as the results were concerned. I gladly approved more budget for the research team once he started making progress in his studies."

Sam's eyes narrowed, recognizing the significance. "Where is this contact now?"

Of course, she would know the schedule and whereabouts of such a strategic contact, but Sam seemed to expect it of her. Perhaps he really was as good as his track record. Forget about evasions then. "He's dining," she said, a trace of mockery in her voice. "While you all scurry about trying to save the city, he is enjoying a meal at an exclusive locale." She gave him the details, and he noted them in his helmet recorder. Then she added, "He does not know it might be his last." She shuddered and looked back at Sam. "I really do want to catch that plane!" she reminded him.

Without any other questions, Sam released her, taking the lead she'd provided. He gave himself 50/50 odds that she would not discover the tracker he had added to her sleeve during the conversation. "Thank you, Director. You might want to find a safer place to hide." Seeing her confusion at his comment, he added with a note of irony in his voice, "That may be difficult, you see. You may not be aware, but the whole world will be in danger from the Titan, not just this city."

With urgency propelling him, Sam activated his suit's thrusters and sped away while Atemiwaza effortlessly ran with him, leaving the Administrative Director and her now-useless escape plan in the dust. The race against time continued, but now, with a sliver of hope.

CHAPTER 35

"IT'S A MARVELOUS KNIGHT FOR A MOON DANCE"

© SYNTHTOPIA #2950

Chapter Synopses: Paint the town Red. It's time to crash a party and find a contact. This upscale event is surely for the social elite. Can the team find their target before it is too late?

The glittering lights of the establishment painted the scene in a fiery red, complemented by the sleek vehicles that littered the entrance. The hum of conversations, soft music, and clinking glasses echoed from within. Red Knight, aka Sam, and Ace, wearing their best attire, stood at the entrance, feeling oddly out of place amid the luxury and ostentation.

"You sure about this, Sam?" Ace whispered, scanning the crowd.

Before Sam could reply, the sound of soft laughter approached them, and they turned to see Artemis, the Moon Maiden. Her ethereal beauty was amplified under the dim lights, making her look even more celestial. Her white gown shimmered as if it was interwoven with moonbeams, and her silver hair cascaded gracefully down her back.

"Sam, you look tense," she teased, giving him a playful wink.

Without waiting for a response, she took his arm, leading him inside. "We have a job to do, after all," she whispered.

Ace and Diana had left Adam and Eve at their safe house, neither in great shape to help with this effort. Adam, formerly Nitro, was too new to the organization for people to trust, and Eve was quite taken with their new relationship. On top of that, their Light and Dark energies were still in a very fragile balance, so it was best that they simply continued to spend time together with as little distraction as possible. On her way here, she had reached out to their society expert, Artemis, to brief her on the situation. She was at home in the high society world and could help.

Ace had also checked in with the Zenith members to get a full workup on the Warlock's contact inside the Yellow Empress' household. His name was Jarrod, and he was not normally the type to sail in these social waters alone. Cipher had found some data quickly, but a full workup required access to the Empress' household systems, and those were adamantine level hardness to crack. It would take time they did not have, so the team opted for a face-to-face confrontation to see if anything would shake loose.

As the trio entered, they were greeted by a massive ballroom, its opulence evident in the gold trimmings, crystal chandeliers, and elegantly dressed attendees. But it was the dance floor that drew the most attention, with couples gracefully moving to the soft rhythm of the orchestra.

Guided by Artemis, Sam soon found himself in the midst of the dancers. Though initially hesitant, he matched her grace, step for step. As they twirled, Artemis used the dance to her advantage, subtly moving closer to their intended contact.

With the swift elegance of a seasoned dancer, she made a seemingly accidental stumble, conveniently falling into the arms of a sharply dressed man—Jarrod.

Sam, playing his part to perfection, feigned embarrassment and excused himself, leaving the two alone.

Jarrod looked at Artemis admiringly. "Your companion should take better care with such a beautiful cargo," he attempted a charming smile.

Artemis raised an eyebrow and gave him a riposte, "I will give you a point on the compliment of my beauty, but take away two points for comparing me to something as…" She appeared to be searching for the right word, "as *mundane* as cargo!" Seeing her target wilt a bit as he realized this was no easy conquest, she took away some of the sting. "Although, I *suppose* I should award you two points for having such great reflexes as to catch me like that!" On came her dazzling smile, and she could see he was back on the hook.

"Seeing that you are ahead on points as of the most recent tally," she continued with a mischievous smile, "it might be an opportunity to suggest we step into the fresh air of the patio so you can comment more on my *beauty* in the moonlight." His lack of recognition reminded her that not *everyone* knew of her title as The Moon Maiden, a title granted both from her appearance and silvery white hair, her regular choice of clothing that responded in various manners under moonlight, and a more esoteric reference to an ancient huntress that only a few were aware of. In any case, his hesitation did not last long. He DID appear to want to see her in the moonlight, alone.

From a distance, Sam watched as Artemis and Jarrod exchanged pleasantries, and it didn't take long before she convinced him to step outside to a secluded patio for some fresh air.

Ace, from her vantage point, signaled Sam that the coast was clear. The Red Knight joined them shortly after they stepped outside, his demeanor shifting from the bashful dancer to a figure of authority.

Jarrod, initially taken aback by the serious expression on Sam's face and assuming that he was about to confront a jealous paramour, soon found himself cornered. Sam and Artemis both confront him. The ethereal glow of moonlight highlighting Artemis's hair made her appear even more otherworldly, further disarming him.

Sam had a hunch that Jarrod really did not know what his part in all this drama really was, so he laid it out for the man. Shock turned to fear, and fear turned to horror. Before that horror could turn into debilitating despair, Sam began digging for answers.

The combination of the impending doom that Sam described and the promise of immunity had Jarrod singing like a yellow canary. He detailed his involvement with the Yellow Empress's vault, his increasing debts as he tried time and again to have a taste of the life that he saw those around the Empress living, and a clandestine meeting with the Warlock at his place of business where he had offered to help Jarrod out. Rather than threaten him, the Warlock commiserated with him about his circumstances and wanted to help him. Moreover, he said that he could go beyond paying off Jarrod's debts; he could give him money to live the life he wanted. The life he deserved. This last part was clearly done under Warlock's mind manipulation. It would not force you to do something against your nature, but it could very easily convince you to go to ridiculous, dangerous lengths for something you secretly wanted.

When Jarrod provided a list of artifacts Warlock had requested, Sam knew they had to act immediately.

Regret was evident in Jarrod's voice as he realized the consequences of his actions. At the end of his narration, he promised to turn himself over to the Empress' security team. He would seek to make amends.

"We need to move quickly," Sam stated to Artemis and Ace on the comm line. To Jarrod, his tone firm, he said, "And Jarrod, remember your promise."

Jarrod nodded, overwhelmed by the evening's turn of events.

As they left the establishment, the glittering red lights seemed to shine even brighter, painting a story of a night and a dance that none of them would ever forget, especially Jarrod.

CHAPTER 36

"IT'S WHAT YOU KNOW AND WHO YOU KNOW THAT DID IT..."

© SYNTHTOPIA #2974

Chapter Synopses: Moon Maiden, Part high society, part rebel, Street name, Artemis. She glides between social layers with ease, if not very discreetly. Still, there is a certain camouflage in her apparently open connection with different groups without any apparent caution or concern. Is she a distraction, a reflection of some brighter light, or does she shine with a light of her own? Rather than prey, is she really a huntress after all?

The vibrant hum of the city's nightlife could be heard from a distance, but in the heart of its pulse, Artemis was a vision of elegance and defiance. Her platinum locks glowed, contrasting sharply with the metallic accents of her ensemble. Every eye was drawn to her, a magnetic force, compelling yet inscrutable.

As she moved through the crowd, her presence was both a statement and a question. The high society elites whispered behind closed hands, their gossip just audible over the din of clinking glasses and soft laughter. "That's Moon Maiden, you know," they'd say, a name synonymous with both reverence and curiosity. To them, she was an enigma wrapped in a riddle, but to the underworld, she was Artemis, a name spoken in hushed tones and hurried exchanges.

Her duality was her strength. Not many could transition from a rebel in the shadows to a beacon in the limelight with such ease. And it was this duality that Artemis would leverage now for a task more critical than any she'd taken on before.

Victoria, the Yellow Empress, wasn't just a figurehead; she was the city's backbone outside of the Mega Corps, her influence reaching the darkest alleys and the loftiest towers. Securing an audience with Victoria was no small feat, but Artemis had something that not many possessed: a treasury of secrets and a network of invaluable relationships.

She approached one of her oldest acquaintances, Lord Belfort, whose mansion was a veritable museum of exquisite art and contraband. With a coy smile, she reminded him of a favor he owed her from years ago. Belfort's hesitation lasted mere seconds before he handed her a gilded envelope, an invitation to the palace. It was for a month hence, but it was a token that she could eventually trade for one with a much more immediate access date.

Next was Lady Evelyn, whose weakness for exotic trinkets had once landed her in a predicament only Artemis could resolve. A brief conversation and a subtle hint later, Artemis secured another card in her favor, this one a valuable piece of intelligence that could make the holder a tidy sum.

By the time dawn broke, Artemis had met with half a dozen of her connections. Some meetings were brief, while others were lengthy negotiations. But with each interaction, her path to Victoria became clearer.

Finally, she met with Mr. Drake. A man whose greed and ambition matched his name. He was due to speak with Victoria this very evening regarding his efforts to obtain an artifact from her collection that rumor had brought to his ears. Normally, nothing could dissuade him from getting closer to an object he had set his eyes on, but the combination of Artemis' many charms, the handful of very profitable opportunities she offered in trade, AND a chance to take a run at the Empress in a month won him over. "A bird in the hand indeed," he thought. Whatever Artimis needed so badly, he was happy to profit from it.

The gates of the palace were grand, guarded by men whose loyalty to the Yellow Empress was unyielding. But as Artemis presented her pass, even they couldn't help but nod in acknowledgment, their stoic faces betraying a hint of admiration. Did Drake sign over his meeting with this woman? Well, not for them to delay a valued guest.

Inside the palace, every step she took was a dance between her two worlds, the luminous Moon Maiden and the cunning Artemis. She was rarely in such close proximity to both high society and underworld bosses. She was usually only accessing one part of her personas at a time. Here, she kept running into people she knew from both worlds, and she found it disorienting, but her focus was unwavering. She was there for one reason, and nothing would stand in her way!

As she finally stood before the Yellow Empress, Artemis took a deep breath. This was the moment. The culmination of all her efforts. And as Victoria's piercing eyes met hers, Artemis knew that the game was only just beginning.

CHAPTER 37

"THE SUN, THE MOON, AND THE STARS"

© SYNTHTOPIA #0880

Chapter Synopses: Yellow Empress, Street name, Victoria, represents a neutral power in the struggle for freedom. With a long line of forbears and a noble house, Victoria runs a vast business empire isolated from the control of mega-corps like Molusk. What is her game, and will she turn out to be friend of foe to the Destabilizers?

Victoria's lair was a confluence of ages. Retro neon signs intermingled with advanced holographic displays. The ceiling, an immense digital sky, showed constellations in ultra-high resolution as they moved in real-time. This was the palace of the Yellow Empress, isolated from the dingy streets of the city, and Artemis was standing right in its heart.

Victoria, surrounded by her council of trusted advisors, looked nothing short of regal. Her cybernetic headdress emitted a soft, golden hue, casting her in a divine light and radiant as a yellow sun, if not so blinding. The chamber went silent as Artemis approached.

"Empress," Artemis began, her voice echoing through the chamber, "I come with grave news."

Victoria raised an eyebrow, her piercing eyes fixing Artemis with a gaze that would have made lesser souls wither. Yet Artemis held firm, as she stated, "An entity known as the Titan was built in a secret lab by the War Twins." This small detail was, in itself, a shock to the room. The War Twins cooperated in different aspects of Molusk Corp operations, but they had a very public rivalry and disdain for one another. Working together, if she was to be believed, was huge news. Knowing she had a lot more to share, Artemis plowed on.

"Not only does this entity have a massive array of physical weapons at its command and bleeding edge self-enhancement capabilities that will make it ever more dangerous, but it has something called a Quantum Emitter that has been integrated into its body. The danger posed by this device cannot be overstated. The inventor," Artemis did not disclose the name as Dr. Haelstrom's reputation may lead the crowd to be skeptical of her warning and not take the situation seriously enough, "suggested that the combination of the latest in modern and now quantum technology would give the War Twins the power to take over, or destroy, the entire world!"

As the room launched into a predictable riot of exclamations and commentary, Artemis stepped as close as security protocols allowed and said quietly for the Empress' ears alone, "The source of the secrets enclosed in the Quantum Emitter is said to be an artifact- one of several, from your own vaults."

Victoria sprang to her feet, astonishment clear on her face, and shouted, "NO! It is IMPOSSIBLE!"

A hush fell over the room at the uncharacteristic outburst. Certain that something extraordinary was happening, the crowd did not want to miss it. The air grew thick with anticipation.

Victoria, unblinking, signaled to her staff and the now curious onlookers, "Leave us," she commanded. They obeyed without question, leaving the two women alone amidst the hum of neon and the soft glow of holograms.

Victoria leaned forward, her voice low, "Years ago, Lady Fortuna prophesied the convergence of the Sun and the Moon in my palace amidst a conflict of the Stars. I had never fully grasped its meaning until now. I pushed her for more details at the time, but she said that the vision had faded from her memory. Apparently, this is not normal and caused her some concern, but that faded as well. I took that as an omen that the prophesy was special."

Victoria paused to reflect on the memory a moment and then continued, "I was curious when my agents told me that you were urgently seeking an immediate audience in such a way that I would not be able to refuse. Your activities are known to me, and I have always held you as an ally for the good of the city, so I have never interfered. As you are aware, my family crest features the Sun in full radiance among its components, so when I heard that the Moon Maiden was seeking to face the Yellow Empress at the palace, the embodiment of the Sun in this place, I became alarmed."

Looking pensive, she continued, "So, if you were not the enemy, you must be a harbinger. Still, the prophesy mentioned Stars."

Artemis listened intently, her heart pounding in her chest.

"Star," Victoria whispered, "was a term the ancients used for a treasured artifact of my lineage. A link to a celestial entity. And if legends hold true, they hold the might of the gods themselves or at least their secrets. It sounds like the Twins might prove that legend true in a very dangerous way."

She rose from her seat, her silhouette dominating the room. "I had always believed there was only one such artifact and that I had it in my possession, and it is based on the ancient artifact that I thought to be safely locked away for the ages. But the Titan's Quantum Emitter... it must be another 'Star.' Thus the prophecy is revealed and our darkest hour is upon us."

As she spoke, alarms began to scroll across her personal console. Without another word, Victoria activated a console. Screens flashed, and commands were sent out. Within moments, the palace was alive with activity. Security teams mobilized, AI drones took to the skies, and her AI-controlled coach roared to life outside.

"This city," she declared, her voice echoing with centuries of authority, "is under the protection of the Yellow Empress. And no force, ancient or modern, will lay it to waste. The Titan", she pointed to the alarms on the console "is making its move and so must we."

Artemis, sensing the gravity of the moment, gave a nod of acknowledgment. The Sun and the Moon had met. Now, the Stars would come together in conflict. She hoped that they would still be around after the collision.

CHAPTER 38

"TRAVELLING COACH WITH CLASS"

© SYNTHTOPIA #0084

Chapter Synopses: The Coachman, a military-grade AI and elite armored transport for the Empress. It coordinates her fleet of security vehicles, weapons, and drones. The Coachman takes its job very seriously and is fiercely loyal as a family retainer in the old sense. It plans on serving the family for a very long time!

The rain streaked the ground, reflecting the neon glow of the city lights. As Victoria stepped into her AI-controlled vehicle, the atmosphere was electrifying. The vehicle itself, The Coachman, was a marvel of technology. Sleek, fortified, and equipped with military-grade AI. This was no ordinary car; it was a moving fortress befitting the Yellow Empress.

As they set off, a notification beeped on the onboard display. "Warlord and Warlock's barricades detected," The Coachman announced in its modulated voice. The AI's sensors immediately picked up a range of threats, blockades, gun emplacements, and a swarm of aerial drones, all converging on them. It appeared that with Warlord absent, Warlock had taken control of both their command structures, again demonstrating a degree of trust and collaboration between the Twins that no one would have believed possible. Tactical analysis from The Coachman indicated that Warlock was trying to prevent anyone from approaching the Titan. They had no doubt that Warlock still expected to "imprint" with the Titan but wanted to be sure that the coast was clear before he did so. The Coachman offered a second-order tactical analysis. Without access to Dr Haelstrom, Warlock may also be uncertain whether it was even safe for him to attempt to imprint. Interesting.

Victoria remained unfazed. "Proceed," she ordered, her voice steely.

The Coachman sprang into action. Its external plating shimmered as dynamic camouflage activated, blending the vehicle with its surroundings. Simultaneously, digital weaponry launched a barrage of electronic countermeasures, sending viral payloads into enemy drones within the closest range of its broadcast wave that could brute force the signal through their filters, rendering them harmless.

The ground shook as barricades ahead were disintegrated by precision laser fire from airborne units controlled by the Empress. Her family had been planning for the security and defense of their interests for generations. Unlike the corporation, which valued efficiency overall and the occasional "secret project" aside, they were not prepared to sustain "security" on the scale Victoria's family was prepared to commit to. Usually, that was reflected in higher profit margins for the corporations, but tonight, it would mean that those who opposed the Empress would be forced to "write off" certain capital assets.

The Coachman nimbly maneuvered around obstacles, its wheels morphing seamlessly to tackle any terrain. The onboard AI was always a step ahead of threats, predicting and neutralizing many of them before they could manifest. The fixed emplacements were as effective as had been expected in the city street grid. That is to say, limited.

When they encountered gun emplacements, the Coachman's exterior emitted a bright pulse, disabling the emplacements' electronics, while plasma canon (definitely illegal outside of military-sanctioned operations) rendered the physical emplacements inoperable. Its advanced targeting systems ensured that each action was surgical and that no civilian was harmed. If any of the people shooting at the Empress were harmed, that was a plus in the Coachman's assessment matrix.

Behind them, a fleet of the Empress's "security assets," advanced drones and automated vehicles, joined the fray, clearing the path and neutralizing Warlord and Warlock minions alike. Their combined might was a force to be reckoned with, ensuring that the Yellow Empress traveled through the chaos unscathed.

The high-speed convoy slowed as they neared the area of the city directly above where Artemis had indicated the secret was buried. It stopped as they reached the area where the Titan loomed. Its presence was ominous, casting a shadow over the part of the city it seemed ready to obliterate. Some minor damage had already occurred, but it seemed mostly to be waiting for something or deciding something. Warlock's imprint effort? Its first decision after being "born"? Artemis was not sure, but she was very concerned that none of the choices would be healthy for any of them.

As the Coachman skidded to a halt, Victoria stepped out, her gaze fixed on the Titan. The Coachman's active combat systems powered down momentarily and entered a more passive monitoring mode, its mission accomplished.

With the path cleared and the threats neutralized, Artemis had time to wonder how Victoria planned on confronting the Titan and prevent impending destruction. The battle for the city, she realized, was just beginning.

CHAPTER 39

"A STAR IS BORN"

© SYNTHTOPIA #0840

Chapter Synopses: Yellow Emitter based on the ancient artifact called a" Star" by the Yellow Empress. Will this version of a Quantum Emitter be strong enough to fight back against the Titan? Will anything?

The soft hum of the Yellow Emitter echoed in the improvised command war room. Its bright yellow glow emanated from the intricate casing, casting dancing shadows on the walls. The machine derived from the ancient artifact, referred to as a "Star" by the Yellow Empress, stood in stark contrast to the advanced machinery surrounding it. The fusion of the past and the present was a testament to the vast knowledge and resources Victoria possessed. It was also a testament to the control she had over her organization, that the existence of this device had been kept secret, and to the discipline she, herself, had not used it for personal gain.

As the Titan began to wreak havoc outside, whatever deliberations it was involved in appeared to be over. It erected a force shield around itself first. The perimeter of the shield was observed as both a coruscating wall of light that swept out from its body along with a wave of debris, signs, vehicles, and other physical objects in its path.

With its body protected, it raised its right hand and, almost tenderly, reached out towards a nearby building. When it clenched its fist, the entire upper section of the building was crushed even though its hand was not close to the destruction or of a scale capable of enclosing the building. Nevertheless, its hand had clearly been responsible for crushing the building from afar.

Cocking its head in a very humanlike gesture, it pointed its left index finger at the top of another building. The upper section fared even worse than the first building, although probably only in absolute terms. This one appeared to dissolve into tiny grains of sand-like material. It was as if it had lost cohesion at an almost molecular level.

Again, the head tilted as it observed the destruction. It paused as if analyzing vast amounts of empirical data from a lab experiment, which it undoubtedly considered these recent actions to be.

It was at this moment that a large caliber weapon impacted the Titan's shield. Looking over to the source, the Titan observed a gun tower (hidden at the top of yet another building) that was the origin of the shots and a whole stream of projectiles (explosive based on the splashes of energy across the defensive shield). The Titan's response was immediate and eminently conventional. A plasma blast larger than anyone on either side of the conflict had ever seen shot out from the Titan's left palm and turned the top of the tower into a hellish inferno.

Satisfied that the threat had been eliminated, it turned its attention back to the particular set of buildings that had its focus previously and tried another of its new and, apparently, untested weapons.

Seeing that the Titan was getting important data from each attempt and that it would retaliate violently to physical attacks, Victoria initiated the Star.

A radiant yellow shield enveloped her forces and the remaining structures, deflecting the powerful quantum blasts. The force was immense, and the shield flickered under the pressure, but it held strong.

Victoria watched intently from her command center, the screens showing the shield's real-time performance. "We have protection against the quantum weapons for now," she whispered, her relief palpable. "But we must find a way to combat its physical form. It may be that it needs to test its weapons to learn how to best utilize them, but this will surely only slow it down. I thought we may be able to neutralize it with this device and that our ground forces might be able to overcome it, but..." she paused as she took in the destruction, "we are just outmatched with the weapons this Titan can wield."

Outside, the streets were in chaos. Warlord's remaining minions clashed with Victoria's security team while the police forces joined in, trying to contain the damage. Buildings outside of the shield still crumbled, streets were torn apart, but amidst the destruction, hope flickered. The shielded buildings stood tall, a beacon of resilience.

But time was of the essence. Every second that ticked by brought them closer to a potential catastrophe. Victoria knew they couldn't rely solely on the Star's power. "We need to find Warlock," she declared, determination evident in her eyes. "He may hold the key to neutralizing the Titan's physical form or have a way to override its destructive programming."

The security team reported in, their voices laced with urgency. "We've identified potential hideouts for Warlock. Our drones are scanning the areas."

Victoria added, "Artemis, I believe your friends may play a pivotal role in this drama. As committed as my forces are to success, your allies may have options I do not. Take news of recent events to them and let me know if they can assist. We will carry on here."

While the security team coordinated their efforts with the police forces and Artemis sped to join with the members of Zenith, the Collaborators, Victoria pondered on the Star's origin. The knowledge of its construction remained a guarded secret within her family. They had deemed the technology too dangerous, a power that could tip the balance of the world. And now, it was their last hope.

As the city's defenders rallied, united in their purpose, a new dawn began to break. The yellow hue of the Star's shield symbolized not just protection but a new beginning. The battle was far from over, but with the Star in play, they had a fighting chance.

Through it all, Victoria planned, gazing at the bright shield, a symbol of hope and resilience, knowing that the true test was yet to come.

CHAPTER 40

"ASK NOT FOR WHOM THE BELL TOLLS..."

Chapter Synopses: Moment of truth, The Red Knight's agent needs to decide what he will do next, and his time, everyone's Time, is running out!

The dense fog of the city, punctuated by the ever-present glow of the streetlights, set the stage for an urgent rendezvous. Nestled in the heart of the city was the iconic central clock, its face glowing like a sentinel. As the clock's minute hand inched towards the hour, Sam and Diana— shrouded in their discreet attire — blended into the shadows, their eyes darting for any sign of their contact.

A lone figure approached, his silhouette highlighted by the clock's light. It was Fletcher, the Red Knight's deep sleeper within Warlock's organization. His gait was hesitant; each step was seemingly weighed down by the immense burden he carried.

Dong

The moment the clock's hand struck the top, a profound bell sound resonated throughout the streets, making Sam and Diana's hearts race in anticipation. Fletcher's eyes darted nervously, the sound amplifying his anxiety.

"Fletcher," Diana whispered, reaching out to steady his trembling form.

Sam, with a watchful eye, surveyed their surroundings, ensuring they were not followed. "We're running out of time," he murmured, looking squarely at Fletcher.

Swallowing hard, Fletcher's voice wavered, "I know what you want, but you have no idea how deep his influence runs. His conditioning...it's intense. You have no idea what it took me, what it took *out* of me, to get into his inner circle."

His mind raced back to when he first encountered Sam. He had been a target of the bounty hunter shortly after Sam's awakening to the dark side of the bounty system. No, he had not been an innocent. Quite the opposite. He was a hardened criminal working for another corporation. The Red Knight's orders had been clear. Terminate on sight. For some reason, Sam had reviewed his file and thought that there might be depths to Fletcher that he himself might not be aware of. It could have been any number of things, individually or together, that caught Sam's attention.

Fletcher had never killed any civilians and even appeared to choose non-lethal options when afforded the opportunity. He was surgical in his approach to crime, yet he helped his elderly neighbor take her trash out. Who knew what calculus had gone through Sam's head? All Fletcher knew was that Sam had the drop on him and decided to go another way. Sam sat him down at gunpoint and made a deal.

Through The Demon, Sam knew that Warlock was looking for someone with a talent for "acquiring" things that were not, strictly speaking, for sale. At this point, Sam still had a lot of connections on the dark side of the business who saw him as dependable, if a bit naïve. With Sam's nomination, he would get the position, and the Warlock's team employees were exempt from bounties other than those given by the Warlock himself. If Warlock needed house cleaning, he usually did it himself.

Fletcher had asked Sam, eyeing the gun still trained on his midsection, "What's in it for you?"

Sam had not wanted to say that he was not willing to be an assassin for hire, so he said, "I think that things are changing. Need to change. I believe that change can only come from inside the system, so I need people on the inside. I want you to be one of those people. I keep you breathing, I keep your secret, and when I call, you answer. That simple."

Fletcher thought that sounded too good to be true, so he said, "Listen, no way someone as high up as Warlock is going to let me run around spilling secrets all the time. I will be watched and useless if they terminate me."

Sam responded, "Oh, it's far worse than that. The word is Warlock puts his people through conditioning. I have some friends that can help prepare you for that. Also, I am not going to be having Tuesday morning breakfast sessions with you. You are going to be silent and deep. I will only be calling when things are serious. If I do, you WILL answer, no matter what. Deal?"

Fletcher chewed on his lip for a minute then, cautiously stuck out his hand and said, "Deal!"

Sam smiled a bit and shook the proffered hand, still looking for any evasion or trick, but Fletcher seemed genuine. His file indicated that he kept his word, and so far, based on his appearance here tonight, that was still true.

With some significant preparation with the Digital Shaman, Fletcher was prepared for his introduction to Warlock's organization. One interesting detail jumped out at Sam as he was taking Fletcher to meet Warlock's representative. He cautioned Fletcher about mentioning any of the people he had met and to put them out of his mind. He simply stared at Sam blankly for a second and then continued with the previous dialogue as if Sam had not said a word. The Digital Shaman had taken care of that already, he thought to himself.

Dong

The clock continued to toll, each chime echoing the urgency of their mission and bringing Fletcher back to the present. Sam, with a firm grip on Fletcher's shoulder, implored, "We need to know. Where is Warlock?"

Tears welled up in Fletcher's eyes as the mental battle raged within him. Warlock's conditioning sought to keep his lips sealed, but the Red Knight's preparations hopefully held a stronger sway. It was a battle of wills, and for a moment, it looked like the conditioning might prevail.

Dong

Then, as the last chime of the clock faded into the misty night, Fletcher, with a voice filled with anguish, barely audible, revealed the location, "The underground lair, beneath the old cathedral. But be warned, it's heavily guarded."

Diana's face paled at the revelation, her hand instinctively going to the weapon concealed beneath her coat. Sam nodded, pulling Fletcher into an embrace. "Thank you. Stay safe."

As the trio disbanded, the bell's haunting echo served as a grim reminder. The hour had come, and the fate of the city hung in the balance. The next move could decide the future, and every second counted.

CHAPTER 41

"HAVE FUN STORMING THE CASTLE"

© SYNTHTOPIA #2912

Chapter Synopses: Warlocks Security at his "castle" where he is hiding. He believes that they are more than a match for potential gate crashers and has his entire arsenal of deceptions ready to deploy as well.

The seedy underbelly of the city pulsed with neon lights, an casting eerie glow on the rain-slicked streets. Within this concrete jungle, the cathedral stood out like a relic from the past, hiding secrets and betrayals behind its ancient walls.

Sam, Diana, and their companion on this hunt, the Paladin, huddled in a nearby alley. Seeming to tower above them, Paladin's armored frame gleamed under the crimson lights, showcasing his advanced biosynth design. He was not like other creations; he was a machine who had defied his creators and their intended purpose. He was a man who had found renewed purpose. His onyx visor turned to Diana, waiting for her signal.

Diana, working feverishly on her portable hacking module, whispered, "Remember, once I send this transport careening into the side of the building, it'll draw their attention. Thanks to the Engineer's remote-control malware, I have full and precise control over the vehicle. That's your window, Paladin. The impact point is calculated to create very little actual damage while still making an impressive amount of noise and a pretty big fireball. In addition to the impact vibrations, sound cover, light burst, and thermal scan cover, I will be using a script daemon from Cipher to kill communications in and out of the building for a brief period. We are relying on you to breach the perimeter, as Warlock is sure to have broadcasting transmitters focused on the entrance to disorient, stall, or otherwise confuse attackers. We will need you to take out the guards and shut down those transmitters! Once inside, I will use the local systems to open an access port for MEO to help as needed."

Paladin's somewhat mechanical voice thrummed, "Understood. My strike will be pure."

Without warning, the ambient hum of the city's electromagnetic chatter was drowned by a sudden silence. Diana had successfully disabled the local comms. "Here goes," she muttered, her fingers dancing across the device.

A distant roar of engines grew louder, culminating in a thunderous crash as an unmanned transport rammed into the aged cathedral's side with sound and fury! Alarms blared, and Warlock's sentinels rushed towards the scene.

It was the moment they had been waiting for.

Paladin, with unparalleled speed, charged forward, his partially metal frame acting like a suit of armor worn by the knights of ancient times. A charged vibro-blade hummed as it powered up. These blades vibrated at a hyper-fast frequency, and the monofilament-edged sword could cut through most normal materials with little resistance. Even laminated graphene shell armor with nano-diamonds sandwiched between the energized layers was merely a hindrance. The sentinels were caught unaware as most attackers would be using projectile or energy weapons that the graphene composite armor could deflect or dissipate.

Paladin knew this and so had devised a simple solution to the formidable challenge in the form of a sword attack. When his allies challenged this apparently suicidal desire to take a "knife to a gun fight", the Paladin had simply shrugged his shoulders and responded, "When one's heart and intentions are pure, they may strike as lighting. Who can stand against the light." He then turned away as if that cryptic response was a perfectly reasonable answer.

The sentinels, even with their envious speed, were caught unawares by the Paladin's assault. The distraction and masking effects had provided the initial cover and element of surprise. To his companions, he did, indeed, seem to strike like lighting, taking down sentinels effortlessly. While they were formidable foes, they were no match for the Paladin's superior combat abilities. He was a force to be reckoned with, unhindered by Warlock's manipulations at the entranceway.

Pausing to disable the Warlock's transmitters, the group came together and moved on.

Sam, close behind Paladin now, fired a series of covering shots, ensuring that no stray sentinels could flank them. "Keep pushing!" he yelled over the noise.

Diana, using the opportunity, maneuvered herself into a strategic position, ensuring that their exit route remained open.

As they breached deeper into the cathedral, they were met with increasing resistance. They had lost the element of surprise, but Paladin never wavered in his assault. Now activating an energy shield on his left forearm and a small plasma pistol in his left hand to compliment the buzzing sword in his right, he leaped, dodged, slid, spun, and hacked his way forward. With every swing of his arm and every pulse of his energy cannon, he cleared the path.

The further they progressed, the clearer it became that they were nearing Warlock's lair. The corridors grew colder, the atmosphere denser. The very walls seemed to echo with malevolent energy as his defensive mechanisms attempted to break their concentration and destroy their will to fight.

Paladin shrugged it all off without apparent effort, even as Sam and Diana used every tool and trick in their arsenal to neutralize the effects.

Sam glanced at Diana, both realizing that the real challenge was yet to come. But with Paladin leading the charge, they had hope.

For now, they had stormed the castle. But the final confrontation with Warlock awaited them.

CHAPTER 42

"WRATH OF THE RIGHTEOUS-FINDING THE PATH"

© SYNTHTOPIA #1425

Chapter Synopses: Paladin, When the pure of heart realize they have been devoted to a corrupt system, they can become its worst enemy. Street name, Chamuel (Cam), his namesake's job was to bring peace and order to the people of the world. As an orphan, he was raised in service to belief only central authority could do that. Until he discovered that central authorities were, ultimately, a reflection of the flaws of those in power. After all, "Power corrupts, and absolute power corrupts absolutely." Perhaps there was another way he could fulfill his life's purpose. Cam is also a biosynth.

The stained-glass windows of the cathedral bathed the sanctuary in a kaleidoscope of colors, painting a contrasting picture of serenity against the unfolding chaos. The Paladin, known on the streets as Chamuel or "Cam," moved with grace and precision. Each strike was delivered with the force of righteous fury, a reflection of the internal turmoil he had wrestled with for years.

The setting they now found themselves in reminded him of his early years. Raised as an orphan and taught that only a centralized power could bring order, Cam had devoted his life to this cause. Yet, with each revelation of the flawed nature of those in power, his faith in the system waned. He had come to understand that true peace and order were more intricate than merely enforcing the will of the few onto the backs of the many.

He learned the dangers of too much power and the old lesson that "Power corrupts, and absolute power corrupts absolutely." He now saw that power needed to be shared in a new way, and so he found his way to the Destabilizers and their Decentralization approach. Still, he was a creature of purpose. If his purpose was not to aggregate power for those who hoarded it like dragons of legend, then his purpose would be to distribute it to the worthy. Thus, he still had a purpose. His life-meaning.

Now, standing against the Warlock and his minions, Cam channeled that purpose, taking down guards with a combination of swift weapon strikes and brutal hand-to-hand combat. The corridors echoed with the sounds of clashing metal and the hum of energy weapons. Each move was a dance, a fusion of his biosynth abilities and his honed combat skills. At the center of it all, he was pure of purpose. While Sam and Diana did not understand what drove Cam, the results were obvious.

Sam and Diana kept pace, using their respective talents to support Cam in his onslaught. Sam was a bulwark on Cam's perimeter by breaking up flanking attempts with his own physical prowess, while Diana played the role of an archer in the antique analog they had formed, taking out any of their opponents trying to line up a shot on her allies from afar. The trio proved to be a formidable force, sweeping through the facility with unmatched ferocity.

Upon reaching the heart of the cathedral, they encountered Warlock in the seat of his power. The room shimmered with a myriad of holographic illusions, obscuring the true nature of their adversary. Shadows danced, and multiple versions of Warlock appeared to also dance, shimmer, and shift, making it nearly impossible to discern reality from fiction.

For the first time since the assault began, the Paladin's focus seemed to prove ineffective. Not only were his strikes hitting only the false images, but their rapid shifting and the distortion field in the air made it impossible to track which ones they had eliminated from the many doppelgangers that seemed to re-appear as quickly as they were discovered.

The team was unaware that none of the images they were looking at were the real Warlock. He was using his camouflage trick to bend light around him and be invisible.

As the team entered an exposed area of the room, the Warlock prepared to launch a cowardly assault on the team from hiding.

MEO, detecting the trap, tapped into the system hack they had initiated upon entering. With a surge of digital energy and frantic instructions, MEO began to wrestle control of the holograms from Warlock, redirecting and repurposing them. It was during the flurry of strange activity that the team saw their danger.

Warlock, momentarily disoriented, struggled to regain control but, in the process, lost control of the projectors that had hidden him. With Sam and Diana providing protection and MEO keeping a lid on the Warlock's arsenal of deceptions, Cam moved in. The Warlock was still a child of War. He had years of secret training with his twin and was a mirror of Warlord's physical perfection.

Warlock attacked Paladin with a series of feints and complex attack patterns and varied his attack timing in mid-strike to throw off Cam. "Still relying on manipulation and deception," Cam commented. "This is who you are. In the end, the pure shall always vanquish the corrupt. Chaos and entropy are the weaknesses that will betray your schemes, as they have NOW!" The last word was punctuated with a brutal and lightning-fast punch through Warlock's guard and into his solar plexus. This stole the air from his lungs and created a hydrostatic pressure spike that briefly stole his consciousness.

Cam stood a moment to process their victory and then approached Warlock. "You believed in the power of manipulation, deception, and control to bring order to this city," he said, his voice resolute. "But true order comes from understanding, compassion, and justice."

Warlock sneered, though trapped and defeated. "You think you've won? This is just the beginning. Without me to protect you, all will be lost. Submit to my rule, and I may yet be merciful." No one believed the lie, even though they believed the threat!

The team used the Warlock's master controls to order the Twins minions to stand down and, hopefully, buy the Yellow Empress some time. Unfortunately, they could not find any self-destruct protocol, even with MEO helping with the search through Warlock's archives. Things were dire. They had to regroup with the others. The search for a means of avoiding a disaster from the Titan would continue, but for Cam, this was more than a mere victory. It was another step on a new path, one where he would bring true peace and order, not through blind obedience to authority, but through righteousness and understanding.

CHAPTER 43

"POWER BEGETS POWER"

© SYNTHTOPIA #2618

Chapter Synopses: Captain of the Guard, Victoria's (Yellow Empress) head of security. She just goes by "Captain". She has worked hard to earn this position and never lets anyone, especially herself, forget her commitment to Victoria!

The temporary command center, nestled deep within the fortress created by the Empress' Yellow Emitter, buzzed with activity. The ambient lighting fluctuated in response to the energy discharges from the outside. On the main viewing screen, the hulking form of the Titan loomed, pulsating with raw energy.

The Captain of the Guard, a formidable figure in gleaming armor, stood before the Yellow Empress, Victoria. Her posture, usually one of unwavering confidence, was tinged with an unease. "Empress," she began, removing her helmet to reveal a face lined with concern, "the Titan is evolving."

Victoria's sharp eyes watched the screen, her face betraying no emotion. "Explain."

The Captain gestured to the live feed, "The Inventor has informed us that the quantum emitter embedded within the Titan is undergoing a metamorphosis along with various *organs* within the Titan. Its structural integrity is reconfiguring at a molecular level. It's like nothing he has never seen."

On the screen, the Titan shimmered, its silhouette distorting and morphing. Waves of destructive energy emanated from the weapons in its arms, crashing against the fortress' protective shield. Each wave was slightly but measurably stronger than the last, the shield flickering and seemingly threatening to fail with every blow. Despite delivering that unending barrage, they could see the shifting shapes along the Titan's torso. Victoria could almost imagine the countless nanobots disassembling and reassembling the Titan as the AI governing its systems analyzed quantum data and the Quantum Emitter's effects and formulated new ways to harness its power.

"Our quantum shield, powered by the Yellow Emitter, is holding," the

Captain continued, "but based on the Inventor's calculations, it will not hold for long. At the rate the Titan is amplifying its power, we estimate less than two hours before our defenses are obliterated."

A heavy silence settled over the command center. The gravity of the situation weighed heavily on the shoulders of every individual present.

"We've faced impossible odds before," Victoria finally said, her voice calm and determined. "We need a strategy."

The Captain nodded, "The Titan's power is formidable, but it must have a weakness. If we can disrupt the reconfiguration process, even temporarily, it might give us the time we need."

An engineer stepped forward, "Your Majesty, if we could introduce a quantum interference pattern, a sort of 'feedback loop,' into the emitter, it could destabilize the Titan's transformation."

Victoria considered the suggestion. "And how do we accomplish that?"

"We have experimental tech, quantum disruptors, that can generate such interference if we can get enough of them in close proximity. They need to be deployed at close range and then fired in a trigger sequence to create the loop effect, which is still purely theoretical. It's risky," the engineer admitted.

The Captain clenched his fists. "Then we'll take the risk. If it means buying more time, we'll do it."

Victoria nodded, her determination unwavering. "Prepare the disruptors. Assemble a team. We have less than two hours and every second counts. We must hope that this will give our allies time to come up with an alternative plan of their own since they have access to resources beyond our reach." She added, "We MUST hold."

The Captain saluted, "Your will be done, Empress."

The command center became a hive of activity, with soldiers and engineers working together, prepping equipment and formulating a plan of attack. The looming threat of the Titan served as a stark reminder of the stakes.

As they prepared for the battle ahead, Victoria stared at the massive form of the Titan, her thoughts clear. They needed more than just a plan. They needed a miracle. And in this dire hour, they would create their own, regardless of the cost.

CHAPTER 44

"A TIME OF REVELATION"

© SYNTHTOPIA #0293

Chapter Synopses: The Engineer. Street Name, Iris. Daughter of The Inventor (Daedalus). Her dad raised her to believe that machines could have a soul. She has worked with machines and systems her whole life, and she has never doubted him. She wondered, however, why stop there? Why not entire systems? Why not cities? Why not a whole planet??? She was about to find an answer, but was she ready for the truth?

In the dim glow of the Zenith team's command center, Iris stood out. The lights played off her high-tech goggles, lending an ethereal glow to her visage. Her gear, an intricate mesh of wires and machinery, seemed to breathe with her, each piece seamlessly integrated into her being. Behind her, a hologram buzzed to life, showcasing the intricate layout of the city's Spirit energy network.

Electra, the ethereal guide who had been with them through thick and thin, floated beside Iris. Her presence was calming, a counterbalance to the chaos outside. "There's truth in your theories, Iris," she began, her voice echoing softly. "The world we inhabit, the very essence of SYNTHTOPIA, is so much more than just physical matter. I wanted you to have more time to discover this yourself. You and your father have made great progress, but we are literally running out of Time!"

Iris nodded, absorbing the gravity of Electra's words. "My father believed that machines have a soul, a consciousness. But why stop at machines? The energy network, the Spirit Nodes, Spirit Hubs, the Towers... they are all part of the underlying energy matrix, so why would it all not have a consciousness?"

Electra's form shimmered, "Exactly. Every tower, every node, they are all extensions of the planet's consciousness, just as we are. It is not aware in the same way that you, synths, biosynths, or we Spirit Animals are aware, but it is a consciousness of a higher order. The quantum foam binds everything, from the smallest particle to the vastness of the cosmos. And within that vast expanse, our collective consciousness rests. As the entirety of the awareness expands in Space, so it can also expand in Time."

The room was silent, everyone hanging on Electra's every word. The battle with the Titan had been a challenge to their understanding of the hidden forces of the universe, but this revelation presented a new, more profound challenge. It seemed that Electra was suggesting that they had to harness the energy and consciousness of an entire planet.

"The Titan threatens to disrupt the harmony, the balance that has been maintained for eons," Electra continued. "Its power grows, but so can ours. We must unite, not just in battle, but in spirit, in consciousness. We can become One," she said with an emphasis that meant far more than just a common purpose. "With our awareness to shape intent, we can prevail, but we must truly become One. Unfortunately, only I can direct the higher-order power and consciousness of the One. I have tried to stay out of direct involvement as much as possible in order to help you all evolve and find your place in the universe, but the Twin's titanic weapon has forced me to intercede. For all of my power," she stated with noble humility, "I cannot stop him on my own. This threat is to the world, and the world must respond to it."

Iris took a deep breath. "Then we connect. We use the Spirit Nodes to link our consciousness through the Spirit Hubs. Every ally, every collaborator, we join as one. As the One," she added, trying to emulate the tone Electra had taken even though she was not absolutely sure what that meant. "Together, we empower you, Electra, to face the Titan."

Electra smiled, a glow emanating from her form. "Together, as One, we will be unstoppable."

The plan was ambitious, but the stakes were too high for hesitation. The team began preparations for connecting to the Spirit Nodes, where each individual consciousness would merge into a collective. The energy in the room was palpable with anticipation. As if in response to the upcoming event, Electra's form grew brighter, more substantial, and more *present*. She was no longer just a guide; she was a beacon of hope and would soon become the manifestation of the planet's will.

The people of SYNTHTOPIA would soon be united in purpose and spirit. They would face the Titan as One, and they ***would*** prevail.

CHAPTER 45

"GOTTA GET YOURSELF CONNECTED..."

© SYNTHTOPIA #0984

Chapter Synopses: A Spirit Hub, hidden on top of one of many buildings, the Hub acts both as a spiritual "lighthouse" and broadcast point to other hubs, nodes, and source locations around the city and the world, or beyond? This network and the access to it that the Spirit Animals, Shaman, and, with the right training and tools, the members of Zenith possess is a key reason for their continued success against mega-corps like Molusk!

Amid the sprawling metropolis, the Spirit Hub stood tall and defiant. Its pulsating glow acted as a beacon in the night for those able to pierce the veil between the physical and spirit realms, drawing in lost souls and energies like a moth to a flame. Its pyramid-like structure gleamed with the symbol of interconnectedness, a representation of the united consciousness they hoped to achieve.

The Digital Monk, surrounded by an array of spirit animals, other monks from his order, and fellow shaman students of Sonic Wage, stood at the base of the Hub, hands raised in concentration. His eyes were closed, but his senses were hyper-aware. He could feel the energy of every individual, every being, every force that wished to join the emerging consciousness of the One.

As the spirit animals began to weave their voices into a melodic soundscape, the monk's mind reached out with his Will, connecting with the myriad allies spread across the city and the world. The sensation was overwhelming at first. It felt like plunging into a vast ocean, where every droplet had a consciousness, a story, a purpose.

Each ally, upon connection, experienced a flash of insight. They saw SYNTHTOPIA from a bird's eye view, a radiant sphere brimming with life and light. They felt the heartbeat of the planet, the rhythm of its rivers, its winds, its soul. And they sensed the presence of each other, a network of energies bound together by a common goal.

But amidst the familiar touch of Synths, Humans, and Spirit Animals, there were unfamiliar signatures. Entities that were hard to define, emanating energies that were foreign yet oddly comforting. They felt ancient, timeless as if they had watched over SYNTHTOPIA for eons.

"Who are they?" whispered a synth from the allies, its voice filled with wonder.

"We do not know," replied a spirit owl, its eyes glowing with the same curiosity. "But they are also with us. They wish to join the One."

The monk, sensing the questions and curiosities bubbling among the allies, spoke up, "It matters not who they are, but what they bring to the One in terms of their intent, their will, their faith in what we are doing. Every consciousness, every bit of energy, no matter how different, has a role to play."

The connections grew stronger, and the network grew wider. The Spirit Hub's light shone even brighter as more and more Hubs connected and energy pathways from the various Sources around the world released ever more energy from other realms into the network, casting away the spiritual darkness that threatened to engulf SYNTHTOPIA in the wake of the Titan's growing power. The energy level was expanding such that it was becoming visible in the physical world. The sense of unity, of being part of something greater, was overwhelming.

As the monk lowered his hands and the spirit animals ceased their chanting, a profound silence enveloped the area, a calm before the storm. The One was growing and evolving, and they were all a part of it now and yet separate at the same time. Whatever lay ahead, they would face it together as One.

CHAPTER 46

"A TORCH TO LIGHT THE WAY"

© SYNTHTOPIA #0711

Chapter Synopses: A candle in the window, a beacon on a shore, a torch to light the way, and hope! Sometimes, the smallest of lights can shine as bright as a star.

Lady Fortuna, known to many as Kizmet, resided in a secluded tower that overlooked the vastness of the city. Its windows, draped with the tapestries of her storied past, barely let in any light. Yet, on this particular evening, a singular candle burned brightly on the windowsill, its flame dancing as if trying to communicate some forgotten lore.

Kizmet gazed at it, her ageless eyes reflecting a deep well of memories, emotions, and knowledge. This candle was not just wax and wick for her. It symbolized hope. In a world where uncertainty had suddenly loomed larger than ever, its light seemed to pierce through the shadow of doubt that had settled in her heart.

For seeming centuries, she had been the oracle of probabilities, weaving the threads of fate with unparalleled precision. Privileged and common folk alike sought her counsel, hoping to gain insight into their future, decisions, and destinies. But now, the intricate web of cause and effect, of choices and consequences, was obscured from her sight.

The question hung heavily in the air: What effect would a butterfly have on a storm? Her unique ability to discern the strange attractors in the chaotic math of future probabilities was close to her. She dared not pierce the quantum foam to the Nexus and Travel as she had so easily done in the past for fear of triggering a catastrophic probability cascade backwards from the future. Never had she felt so isolated, powerless, and alone.

Sitting at her grand wooden table, surrounded by the relics of a time gone by, Kizmet contemplated her newfound uncertainty. Would the merchant who frequented her chambers arrive tomorrow with a pouch filled with gold, seeking her wisdom? Would the child, playing in the streets below, pick up the fallen feather of a raven or a dove? Realizing that in her stress, she had started thinking in ancient analogies, she chided herself. Pouches? Feathers? It's more like credit sticks and artifacts of the modern era.

A sigh escaped her lips. Such simple things, previously clear in her mind's eye, were now veiled in mystery.

Yet, amidst the uncertainty, she felt calm, focusing on her candle. She felt a pull, an inexplicable connection beckoning her towards unity. The collective consciousness of the One reached out to her like whispers carried by the wind, urging her to become part of something bigger, something profound.

She heard a chant, a song, a promise beckoning to her. It was both ancient and new and reverberated with the echoes of the cosmos:

It abides deep inside, born to ride the Wind;

Break the spells, these chains that bind;

Let's Begin Again!

I don't know just where we'll go; Don't know where it ends.

But when we're done, we will be One.

Let's Begin Again!

Born in Flame, He called my name And turned night into day.

A gift of sight, a beacon bright,

A torch to light the way.

I don't know just where we'll go; Don't know where it ends.

But when we're done, we will be One.

Let's Begin Again!

Born to walk upon the Earth; Sent forth among these men,

The lost to find, to make them mine.

Let's Begin Again!

I don't know just where we'll go; Don't know where it ends.

But when we're done, we will be One.

Let's Begin Again!

Water pure, to heal and cure; to wash away all stain!

An end to strife, Begin new life!

Let's Begin Again!

I don't know just where we'll go; Don't know where it ends.

But when we're done, we will be One.

Let's Begin Again!

Oh, Let's Begin Again!

Kizmet, drawing strength from the candle's unwavering flame and the song that called to her, made her choice. With closed eyes and open heart, she sent forth her energies, laden with hope and faith. She relinquished her need for foresight, embracing the present moment and the collective spirit of SYNTHTOPIA.

As the last remnants of her awareness merged with the One, the candle's flame flickered momentarily, casting shadows that danced like ethereal spirits on the walls. The Oracle of Probabilities, in her act of faith, had become a beacon of hope, guiding others to find their own light within the darkness.

CHAPTER 47

"THE HEART OF THE CITY"

© SYNTHTOPIA #0040

Chapter Synopses: the Spirit of the City is rising. SYNTHTOPIA rises to fight against tyranny and destruction. What changes are in store in the aftermath?

Amidst the vast expanse of jagged mountains and misty valleys, the city stood tall and resilient, a beacon of technological marvels in an age of wonders. Its towering spires, pulsing with neon lights, seemed to touch the heavens, while its depths seemed to plumb the very core of the planet. It wasn't just a cluster of buildings, pathways, and machines; it was a living entity, attuned to every heartbeat, every whisper of its denizens.

The One, a collective consciousness that had been growing in power and reach, had woven its essence into the fabric of the city. And as the One expanded, drawing more beings into its fold, the city stirred, feeling the weight of the responsibility it now bore.

Deep within its central core, a magnificent chamber pulsated with energy. The walls, made of a shimmering, translucent material, reflected a myriad of colors, painting a vivid tapestry of life. And in the center, suspended in mid-air, was a shimmering, glowing entity in the shape of a tigress: Electra.

The city spoke to Electra, not in words but through raw, unfiltered emotions. The emotions of every being, every creature that had ever existed in its vast expanse. The love of a parent for a child, the anguish of loss, the joy of discovery, the fear of the unknown. Every sentiment was laid bare before her, creating a bond so profound that words could not capture its depth.

Electra sensed the impending danger, the discord threatening the very harmony of existence. The Titan, a formidable adversary, was not driven by its own malice but by the malicious intent of its programming. The growing threat it posed, however, was not a bit less dire for all that.

The city, drawing from the collective will of its inhabitants and the force of the One, empowered Electra. She was no longer just a Power of Spirit and

Electrons but the embodiment of the city's spirit, its heart. The primal force of a mother protecting her offspring surged through her. She was ready to face the Titan, not with animalistic fury but with the fierce determination to safeguard her home and her people.

In the blink of an eye, Electra materialized in the area where the Titan was attempting to wreak havoc, and the Yellow Empress and her people were giving everything; they had to hold it back, knowing that it would not be enough. Electra nodded and noted the nobility of their purpose and was determined their efforts would not be in vain.

With every step Electra took, the city resonated with her, amplifying her intent. The buildings shimmered, the streets vibrated, and the air crackled with energy. Time seemed to blur, with past, present, and future converging into a singular moment of infinite possibilities.

The heart of the city had awoken, and with Electra as its champion, it was prepared to shape the destiny of SYNTHTOPIA. Together as one, they stood in an unbreakable union against any force that threatened their harmony. The city, its people, and Electra, intertwined in an eternal dance of life, were ready to reclaim their peace.

CHAPTER 48

"TIGER, TIGER- BURNING BRIGHT"

Chapter Synopses: Icarus Tigris (Spirit Tiger) is a friend to the Virtual Shaman, the Hacker Cipher, and an agent of change in SYNTHTOPIA and goes by the Street name Electra. In ancient times, she would have flames or antlers, but in the modern world, this powerful white tigress has merged the spirit world with the cyberspace realm of electrons. Powerful in both physical and digital realms, she may be the ally the Destabilizers need to awaken SYNTHTOPIA and reach their true home.

In the neon-lit streets of SYNTHTOPIA, legends whispered about Icarus Tigris, a spectral figure embodying both ancient mysticism and modern digital prowess. By the street name Electra, she was a revered emblem of transformation—a bridge between the spiritual and virtual worlds.

Electra's form shimmered between that of a powerful white tigress and a cybernetic entity, gracefully navigating the spectrum between the physical and digital. In older times, her fiery mane and antlers would signify her prominence in the spirit world. But now, in this age of bytes and pixels, her essence was etched in circuits, glowing vibrantly against the dark alleys of SYNTHTOPIA.

When the Virtual Shaman and the Hacker Cipher first summoned Electra, they realized they had called upon a force far beyond their comprehension. Her presence was electric, filling the room with a palpable tension—a raw, unbridled energy that resonated with their core intentions. They felt her ancient wisdom and modern prowess, making her the ideal ally for the Destabilizers in their mission to awaken SYNTHTOPIA. It was only later that they learned that their "summoning" was really just the realization of a set of probabilities that Electra herself had manifested. In short, they called her because they needed to call her, and she came because that was her destiny.

For a Power such as herself, she simply accepted the dictates of Fate and Purpose and went about helping the Collaborators and Destabilizers in ways that they could accept and comprehend, for only by encouraging foundational growth would their roots be strong enough to face the corruptive forces of greed and temptation.

The threat of the Titan loomed large, casting a dark shadow over their hopes. But Electra was undeterred. She merged with the collective spirit known as the

One, absorbing the will and intent of every being united in their purpose. The amalgamation was profound, and what emerged was an entity of unparalleled might.

As the Spirit and quantum energies came to that place and time, it was as if the rest of reality, past and future, became a dream, a memory. It was as if this moment was the Big Bang, the origin of all things that were or would be, and it seemed that the whole universe could be unraveled and rewritten from this point to begin again as something else. Electra, with the One, realized that this was the danger. She and the collective One would need to carry the history and future of the Universe with them through the fight and beyond so that it might re-establish itself on the other side of the conflict. They could not just win; they had to be flawless in their victory!

As they confronted the Titan, a blinding spectacle unfolded. Electra's form radiated with ethereal light, and her intent took shape as a paw full of colossal claws imbued with the power of annihilation, ethereal yet devastatingly real. The Titan, a monument of power in its own right, was caught off-guard, unprepared for the wrath it was about to face. Nothing in its programming prepared it for another being on this level of pure power, nor could its sensors understand what they were seeing.

As the Titan sought to bring its full arsenal of massed destruction against this new threat, Electra's claws, imbued with the collective force of the One, slashed through the Titan, tearing it apart molecule by molecule. At a quantum level, the Titan was unmade, its existence erased from the very fabric of reality.

Lady Fortuna had been right. With enough force, the boundaries of time could be transcended. As the Titan disintegrated, the quantum principles it was built upon began to unravel. Its connections spread across every conceivable WHEN and WHERE, snapped. The Warlocks' research, the foundation of the Titan's might, was obliterated from existence. Unfortunately, this was only a partial unraveling, and the lives lost and the damage done remained.

In the settling dust of the battle's aftermath, a scarred and wounded SYNTHTOPIA emerged. Though the immediate threat had been neutralized, the repercussions of the Titan's brief reign lingered. Electra, alongside her allies, knew their work was far from over. A great deal of knowledge had been given to those who might not have been ready for it. New beings that had been thought to be myths have been connected to the people of SYNTHTOPIA. Scientists might not have the Warlock's research, but history has shown over and over that once people knew something was possible, they eventually figured out how to do it, whether they should or not.

In the meantime, they had a city to rebuild and a future to reshape, but with unity and determination, they were ready to embark on this new chapter.

CHAPTER 49

"BY THE PRICKLING OF MY THUMBS"

Chapter Synopses: Behind Closed Doors, the new Executive team waits for Tyrannus. No stranger to power politics and cutthroat bureaucracy, this team is about to discover a whole new level of play. They better be up for the challenge!

The chamber was awash in a soft, eerie glow. The colossal table around which they sat reflected the tension in the air, almost palpable. Faint hums of electronic devices, the soft rustling of paperwork, and the barely audible murmurs of conversation echoed through the cavernous and well-appointed room. But amidst the sea of trepidation, one figure was conspicuously calm, watching with calculating eyes. Tyrannus.

Each member of the Interim Executive Team sat with a posture of suppressed anxiety, their eyes darting around, searching for a sign, a clue, anything that might hint at the fate of their predecessors. Rumors were rife—some whispered of covert terminations, while others spoke of shadowy prisons where executives were put 'on ice.' The tales were countless, and each one was more chilling than the last.

Yet, within this room of uncertainty, there was also a glint of ambition. This was the seat of power for the Molusk Corp, and the entire room and the building around it were built as a testament to the absolute authority wielded by the head of the organization. Within that corporate structure were built-in positions of power. It is not absolute per se but an extensions of power that could be shaped.

For some, the mysterious disappearance of the previous executive team was an unexpected opening—a crack in the previously impenetrable wall of power erected by N1ght T3RrOr and the War Twins. The ambitious ones saw this as their chance to ascend, to wield the power they had only dreamed of.

Tyrannus leaned back, his metallic armor gleaming under the dim lights. His piercing gaze swept over each member of the team, silently assessing their worth. The air grew colder with every passing second, but Tyrannus reveled in it. These replacements, in his eyes, were but mere shadows of the original team. Yet, he thought, they might prove entertaining.

"Times of uncertainty," Tyrannus began, his voice deep and resonant, "often reveal the true nature of beings. You sit here today, not because you were the first choice, but because destiny has handed you a chance."

He paused, letting the weight of his words sink in. "The Titan, in all its destructive glory, has left our competitors scrambling. Chaos reigns outside these walls, and chaos," he grinned slyly, "is an ***opportunity***."

There was a collective intake of breath. Tyrannus continued, "It is time to exploit this situation, to drive profits to greater heights, and to claim the dominion that rightfully belongs to us. Fail, and you might just find out what happened to the *last* executive team." The way he intoned the word "last" sent chills down the spine of every person present.

He leaned forward, the light catching the menace in his eyes. "Now, let's get to work."

As the team members hurriedly began discussing strategies, Tyrannus reclined in his chair, amused. He would give them enough rope to see what they'd do with it. And in the shadows of SYNTHTOPIA, the game was afoot once more.

CHAPTER 50

"WHEN WE'RE DONE, WE WILL BE ONE"

© SYNTHTOPIA #1602

Chapter Synopses: Zenith, aka "the Collaborators." Former corporate executives who have turned against their employers and now provide the Destabilizers with valuable intel and resources. They now gather in the aftermath to reflect on recent events and what it all means for them and for SYNTHTOPIA!

Amidst the sprawling landscape of the metropolis, a tranquil hush had fallen. The once bustling streets were now cloaked in a gentle silence, save for the whispering winds that carried tales of resilience and rebirth. Above, the neon skyline painted a serene picture, contrasting the chaos and upheavals of yesterday.

The Collaborators, fondly called Zenith, stood tall and defiant, casting long shadows on the rooftops. Once powerful executives in the corporate realm, their roles had transformed. Their silhouettes, etched against the backdrop of the city, told a story of redemption and revolution.

Each member of Zenith bore the scars of betrayal—betrayal by their former employers, former alliances, and, at times, betrayal of their own conscience. But from those scars emerged a determination to mend the broken fabric of society, to be the beacon of hope in the darkness.

As they gazed over the city, memories of their union with the One flooded back. It was an experience beyond words—where individuality melded into a singular force, an energy that surged through them, connecting every fiber of their beings. In that ephemeral moment, they had tasted the limitless potential of unity, an overwhelming sensation of being bound together in purpose and spirit, and yet never lost their individuality. They had come away with a greater purpose and a shared hope that surpassed the slender candle that once burned for them individually and had become a bright torch, a lighthouse beacon that they could all follow together.

"Our journey has only just begun," mused The Digital Monk, his hardened form and calm voice projecting power and conviction. His voice was low but carried through the assembled allies. "We've discovered the true essence of our collective power. What we felt with the One... it's a testament to what we can achieve."

Moon Maiden, with her vibrant hair and piercing gaze, nodded. "We've liberated this city from the clutches of corruption. But more than that, we've ignited a flame within its people. They've seen what's possible when we stand united."

Daedalus, the tech genius of the group, added, "We've defeated the forces that sought to centralize and control. But the real work begins now building a society where every individual thrives, where collaboration overpowers competition."

The rest of the Collaborators shared knowing glances, reflecting on the enormity of their achievements and the path that lay ahead. Their journey with the One had shown them a glimpse of an ideal world, a world they were now determined to build.

As dawn began to break, casting the first rays of sunlight onto the city, the Collaborators stood together, hand in hand, embodying the spirit of unity. The challenges ahead were many, but they were ready.

For in their hearts, they knew that when they were done, they would truly be *One*.

ABOUT THE AUTHOR

Victor Newsom (aka LordElvic), a long-time book lover, gamer, and avid fan of art and science, has four grown children and lives on a mountain with his wife and "grand kitten." Victor holds multiple patents, a Black Belt in Taekwondo, a multitude of tattoos, has appeared in Bodybuilding (Iron Man), FinTech, and Gaming magazines, and is known to present at conferences where he will talk at length about technology innovations in payments and crypto (whether you ask him about it or not, you have been warned). This first book was inspired by the NFT collections, artwork, community, and goals of the SYNTHTOPIA project and the Destabilizers.

Find out more at www.synthtopia world

ABOUT SYNTHTOPIA

SYNTHTOPIA is a Transmedia IP Franchise at the forefront of the creative industries. We blend AI-driven content with gamified entertainment, harnessing the power of Web3 and the Metaverse.

Our mission is enlightening and inspiring, as we explore the untapped potential of emerging creative technologies while capturing the evolving cultural dynamics of our era. We empower artists, creators, and our greater community, enabling them to monetize their work via our IP franchise. Integral to our mission is the 'Synthesis Reward System,' a novel approach to incentivize and meaningfully reward participation and creative contributions.

Our role transcends beyond just offering a platform; we are fostering a vibrant, collaborative movement that champions innovation, community, and artistic expression. SYNTHTOPIA is more than a revolution in the creative industries — it's about shaping a future where creativity, technology and community seamlessly converge.

Be part of the creative movement at www.synthtopia.world

THE CHRONICLES OF
SYNTHTOPIA

www.ingramcontent.com/pod-product-compliance
Lightning Source LLC
Chambersburg PA
CBHW070838020826
48982CB00021B/1474/J
* 9 7 9 8 9 8 9 9 5 4 3 4 6 *